Impressions

Barbara Winkes

For D.

Chapter One

*I*t was almost time to meet her. Putting together each detail was the hardest part. Every small mistake could become the thread that unraveled the whole picture—but she didn't make mistakes. Enjoying a last coffee before the big moment, she smiled to herself, thrilled with the prospect of reuniting with the person that had always been missing in her life. It felt incredibly real, and it would be even better...as long as it lasted. The sad part was that nothing could last forever, but if she was good enough, she could stay for a while. Be the person she was meant to be.

Jordan and Derek had left almost immediately after they'd arrived at the station. For Ellie, the day began a bit more relaxed as she was catching up with paperwork and messages left in her absence. Her partner Cliff Waters was nowhere to be seen, and she wasn't about to look a gift horse in the mouth. Mid-morning, Detective Maria Doss went on a coffee run and stopped by Ellie's desk for a break and some conversation.

"So, do tell," she said, taking the visitor's chair. "How was the honeymoon? Didn't you regret not taking more days off?"

Life had been busy leading up to those perfect moments, so Jordan and Ellie had agreed to take a prolonged weekend at a spa retreat rather than a longer trip.

"Oh, no, it was amazing," she said. "Thanks, by the way." She picked one of the hot beverages and opened the lid. "Caramel latte. It's not so bad coming back to this—though I really loved it. The nature, and fireplaces everywhere...Even the naps were tantric."

She didn't notice her choice of words until Maria started laughing.

"Transcendent. That's what I meant."

"Still, too much information, and a bit cruel to the single lady."

"I'm really sorry."

"Don't worry. I can take it." Maria took a sip of her coffee. "You better enjoy the peace and quiet while you can. Cliff's been grumbling the whole time...When he was actually present, that is. Funny how in his opinion, only the women have too much off time."

"He said that?" Ellie frowned. "We had a vacation last year, and before that, I never took more than a couple of days at the time. I know Jordan did the same. What's his problem?"

"The whole world," Maria commented. "Anyway, I'm glad you had a good time. It's been almost quiet...you know that never lasts long."

"True." After the past few days, Ellie felt fairly ready to face whatever was going to come her way. Besides enjoying the heavenly tranquility of the mountain spa, including sauna, massages, and the hot tub, she and Jordan had talked, a lot more than during those days in Hawaii, when they'd still had so much healing to do. Many things had still been uncertain back then. Now they had a solid foundation that enabled them to look at everything that had led them here.

"Harding, where's your partner?" She turned around to face Lieutenant Carroll who had left his office.

"I don't know. I haven't seen him today." Ellie barely suppressed a wince when she saw the irritation in his expression.

"All right, then, Doss, you go with her."

"Sir...I have a meeting with the D.A. in..." Maria checked her watch. "Seven minutes. I should be going."

"That's okay. I can go by myself," Ellie offered. Much to his credit, Carroll only hesitated for a brief moment.

"Sure. Arnold Robertson, the music producer, was just found dead in his condo by his bodyguard."

Ellie was already standing, keys in hand. "I'm on my way."

Peace and quiet were over.

❦

Officers Chris Atwood and Samantha Potts were on the scene, and a perimeter around the building had already been established. Ellie had to make her way through a crowd of press and bystanders.

"You're late," Atwood said, and she barely refrained from rolling her eyes. Atwood was about the only friend Waters had in the department. While he was younger than Waters, his antiquated ideas were even worse than the detective's. He didn't like that Ellie had made this step up the career ladder, either.

At the front door, she showed her badge to a concierge who studied it for an inappropriate length of time, and on the penthouse floor, a guard quickly followed her.

"Ma'am, you can't go in there."

"I believe I can," she said, flashing her badge again. "Thank you."

The apartment stretched over two floors, with floor to ceiling windows. Ellie had no time to admire the view, her gaze drawn to the body in the center of the room. In another corner, Casey Lyons was talking to a burly man Ellie assumed to be the body-guard, and ME Melissa Adams was taking pictures.

Now was not the moment to get nervous. She had proven that she deserved to be here, she knew what to do, and most of all, it wasn't her fault if Waters neglected his duties to the point no one could ignore it any longer.

She walked over to Dr. Adams, grateful no one but herself could hear her heart that was beating loudly all of a sudden.

"Good morning, Doc. What do we have here?"

"You're aware of *who* it is we have here, right?" Dr. Adams asked dryly.

"Yes, of course. Arnold Robertson, the music producer. I've heard of him, but I didn't know he lived in the city."

"Well, someone who didn't like him very much knew. By the way, there's a woman in the other room they found holding this," she held up a gun enclosed in an evidence bag. "Her shirt's soaked in blood."

For a brief moment, Ellie wondered if it could really be this easy. She looked down at Robertson who had been shot mul-tiple times. How had that woman made it past the bodyguard? Unless...

"The how is pretty obvious, right?"

"I'd be surprised if those bullets didn't come from this gun," Melissa said.

"Okay, let's find out."

She knew Melissa would want to know if her team could move the body. Ellie saw no reason why not, given the rather clear circumstances of how Robertson died. She wanted to talk to the bodyguard and see the woman before they brought her to the station, wishing she could do everything at the same time—wishing her partner would take the job more seriously.

Still being the newbie in the Homicide unit, she couldn't afford to make mistakes.

"That means we can go ahead? Detective?"

"Yes. Call me as soon as you know more."

Ellie walked over to Casey Lyons and the man she was talking to.

"This is Raymond Owens, Mr. Robertson's bodyguard. He found him earlier."

"I also found the bitch that did it," Owens said angrily. "Are you going to remove her from this house, or what?"

Ellie sent an imploring look to Casey who supplied the information she was looking for. "Her name is Brandi Gilbert. She'd been a guest of Mr. Robertson's a couple of times before. Those visits passed without incident, Mr. Owens told me."

"She's a hooker, if you must know. It's obvious that she was after money, probably to pay for drugs."

"We'll get to the bottom of this," Ellie assured him. "In the meantime, I'd like to talk to you at the station, just so we can clear up some things."

"What's to clear up? I saw her with the gun in her hand."

"She threatened you?"

He seemed almost offended at that. "I disarmed her, and then I made sure she stayed put until the police arrived."

So that was what Atwood had meant when he said she was too late. Well, neither Atwood nor Owens would decide the next steps.

"Okay. I'll meet you at the station. Thank you for your co-operation."

In an office off the main living area, Brandi Gilbert sat, sobbing, the officer in the room with her shaking her head.

"Has she said anything?" Ellie whispered.

"No."

"Ms. Gilbert? I'm Detective Harding. Can you tell me what happened here?"

The woman looked up at Ellie with so much despair in her expression she felt a chill run down her spine.

"Have you arrested him yet?"

"Who?"

"Ray...if that's his name." She sounded nauseated, but that might be from the blood soaking her shirt. It made Ellie think of her first case...Bloody clothes didn't always mean someone was guilty. On the other hand, she might be trying to shift the blame.

"Are you saying that Mr. Owens shot Mr. Robertson?"

She cast a frightened look towards the door, then shook her head.

"I did it," she said.

On her first day back at work after her honeymoon, Ellie was apparently having it all: The murder weapon, and a suspect confessing at the drop of a hat.

Nothing was ever this easy.

⁂

On her way back she tried to call Waters but didn't reach him. Fortunately, the D.A. had cut Maria's meeting short, and she could make some time to set up a room for Owens and Gilbert each. Ellie wanted the blood on the latter's clothes tested against Robertson's, and have her hands tested for residue.

Next, she called A.D.A. Esposito. It was strange to think that she, albeit for a short time, had felt jealous of the woman, Jordan's ex. It was all about work. She needed to do things in the right order, learn what she could from Owens and Gilbert, to make sure charges would stick. Ellie was aware that she would hardly ever get a better suspect than a person literally holding the smoking gun. She still felt a bit uneasy, unsure if they might get any bad surprises from Owens.

However, when she arrived at the station, he had grudgingly agreed to wait in the room Detective Doss had showed him. Ellie took another few minutes to update Lieutenant Carroll, and then she stepped into the room where Owens was sulking over his coffee.

"I still don't understand why I had to come here. I already told everything to the officer who was first on the scene."

"Yes. I'm sorry about the inconvenience. When did you enter the apartment today?"

"Around nine-forty-five. Mr. Robertson had called me."

"Did he sound like he was in distress?"

"No. He wanted me to come over and take care of something. He didn't say what. This is ridiculous. None of it has anything to do with—"

"Mr. Owens, please. The sooner we get this done, the sooner you can go."

"You can't keep me here. I haven't done anything."

"If you could tell me what happened when you arrived at the apartment. You have keys?"

"Yes. I let myself in, and saw Mr. Robertson right away, bleeding on the floor. The bi—Gilbert was crouching next to his body, the gun still in hand. Hell, how much more do you need? She must have shot him five times at least."

"You didn't see her shoot him or heard the gunshots."

He shook his head, exasperated. "I didn't need to."

"You told my colleague that she'd been to Mr. Robertson's place a couple of times. Did he often bring home sex workers?"

"What are you saying, that it was his fault the slut killed him?"

Lots of anger, Ellie thought, but Owens didn't seem to grieve all that much for his boss.

"I'm trying to get the whole picture."

"Then let me help you. Arnold always kept wads of cash with him. She must have noticed that before and thought she could make a quick buck."

"The gun is his?"

"I don't think so, but that's your job to find out. Whenever you find the time to get back to it," he sneered.

"Oh, don't worry, Mr. Owens, we'll make the time we need. Thank you. We'll be in touch." Ellie got up to reach out a hand. To her surprise, he shook it in a grip tight enough to make her wince. "Mr. Owens. Just one more thing. Who was responsible for bringing the women there?" Her use of plural was no slip of the tongue, and he didn't correct her.

Owens shrugged. "Not me. I suppose he used some escort service. You have means to find out, don't you?"

"Definitely. Thanks again."

Ellie took a deep breath after he'd left the room, but she didn't have much time to think about what she'd just heard, or her next step. The door was yanked open, and Detective Cliff Waters stepped inside, A.D.A. Esposito in tow. She looked uncomfortable and apologetic.

"Harding, why are you wasting your time with this guy? You have a person who confessed, drenched in the victim's blood. Do I have to do everything around here myself?"

"She gave contradicting statements. I thought it was important—"

He had already turned around and left.

"I hate to say it, Ellie, but this time he actually has a point."

Ellie shook her head as she closed the door, walking along the hallway with the A.D.A.

"I don't know. That woman is clearly traumatized."

"That doesn't mean she didn't do it."

"Yeah." Ellie sighed. "I think she should see a psychiatrist before the judge."

"She'll have a public defender who'll determine if they consider it necessary."

Ellie wasn't convinced, and most of all she was angry with Waters for swooping in and taking over like that. She wondered what the lieutenant would have to say about it.

Chapter Two

I n another apartment across town, Jordan walked into a modest two bedroom, barely furnished. A neighbor had called the police after hearing gunshots. Two men, both late thirties to mid-forties, both shot in the head. The image quickly did away with the glorious memories she'd carried with herself up to this moment. The wedding. The honeymoon. It seemed unreal in the face of this precisely carried out violence. She was surprised to see an ME she wasn't familiar with.

"Dr. Adams isn't here?"

"Nope, busy on the other side of town with the Robertson murder. The music producer," he said when Jordan didn't react right away. "You might have heard of him, he had his studio here for a few years."

It was when Jordan realized she'd read a story about him once.

"A bit more high-profile," she said.

"Yeah," he confirmed. "Quite the violent start of the week."

"No kidding. So, what can you tell me about these gentlemen so far?"

"At this moment, not much more than what meets the eye. GSW to the head, from up close." He pointed out the barely visible indentation in the skin around the wound, indicating that the killer had pressed the barrel against the back of the head. "Same with the other one."

"All right, thanks." She walked towards the window, careful to stay away from any blood spatter. Seeing the name of the bar on the other side of the street, she had an idea. There were a couple of people she could ask for a theory of what had happened to these men.

Derek joined her by the window. "Time to talk to a few people in the neighborhood?"

"Definitely, but first I want to see what we can find here. Not the murder weapon, that much is for sure. This was done by a pro."

"I agree. I hope you had a great time, because the honeymoon is definitely over."

"No kidding." She suppressed a sigh. "But yes, it was great." It didn't seem right to bring anything about the past few days into this room, so she hurried to change the subject. "I want to know what they made money with. Being where we are, my guess is drugs or prostitution. Their clothes don't look like they're regular residents either."

Uniformed officers were already starting the search, Libby Marshall among them. Jordan and Derek went into the first bedroom. Like the other room, it was sparsely furnished, with only a bed, a table and a chair. There were cables lying on the floor, USB, she noticed. The electronic devices that went with them were either well hidden, or the killer had taken them.

Jordan carefully opened the door to what could qualify as a walk-in, and stepped back immediately. She had noticed a strange combination of smells in the room, but in there, it was condensed: The floor of the closet was littered with food containers and soda cans, the smell mixing with that of perfume or some other product. A mattress was wedged into the small space. Jordan didn't dare guess what some of those stains might be. She did guess that the two men had held someone in there. They were likely to get DNA and fingerprints, though she worried there might be too many for conclusive results.

"Okay, this just took a turn to worse," Derek remarked. Before he could go into detail, Libby called from another room.

"Jordan? Could you come here for a moment?"

Glad to turn away from the nauseating sight, Jordan went to join her, the conflicting theories already giving her a headache. There had been another person in the room, obviously. They might have killed the men, or someone had done it on their behalf, but either way, it didn't fit the idea of a hit carried out by a professional. All of it hinted at more conflict to come.

"We found something," Libby told her, pointing to lose bricks in the wall. Behind them was a stash of cash, several ten-thousands of dollars, Jordan guessed.

"Whoa. That looks like Mr. Hart was no saint. This was in the dresser." Derek held up a wallet with the ID of a Ted Hart. "No ID on the other one, but it's a start."

"That and almost a hundred thousand dollars. Could be drugs or prostitution, maybe both."

"That's yet to be determined, right?"

Everyone turned around at the sound of her voice. The woman with the brown hair and the soft voice was wearing an FBI windbreaker.

"Ladies and Gentlemen...I'm Special Agent Nina Torres. We will need everything you found on these men. We appreciate your cooperation...and as for your case, we'll be glad to help any way we can. Detective..."

"Carpenter," Jordan said, hoping she hid her surprise well enough. "You talked to Lieutenant Carroll already?"

"Right before I came here," Torres confirmed. "He set me up with the necessary resources. We can talk in my office later."

"It looks like they held someone here. The money could be a ransom."

"It's possible, but I'm not certain of that yet. Like you said before, they could have been involved in risky business. I'm aware you made great progress when you recently put away Bud Ryder, and Ryan Lemont, but there's always people trying to carve out a niche for themselves."

"We are keeping an eye on that."

"Good. Nice to meet you, Detectives. I need to have a word with your ME now. Please, find me later at the station."

"I guess we have no choice," Derek mumbled once she was out of earshot. "They are all the same, aren't they?"

Jordan didn't think he expected an answer, so she didn't give one. In fact, she thought Nina Torres was very different from her ex, a psychiatrist and oftentimes FBI liaison for the department. Torres seemed to be a bit more...low-key, trying to form connections.

She thought that a low-key relationship with the FBI would probably be to their mutual benefit. Bethany had happily moved on after her promotion, only coming back to town once to testify.

"I think we're going to be okay," she said. "Let's go see our new friend Mulveney on the way back." Not much went on in this neighborhood that people wouldn't talk about at *Rigley's*.

<hr />

On the way downstairs, a woman passed them by, and it took Jordan a split-second to remember where she knew her from. She turned around quickly.

"Ms. Geller, hello."

Kim Geller had once led them to the man they were going to see. Coincidence? It seemed a bit much.

"Detective. I still have your card, but there wasn't any reason to call...until now, I guess, but one of my neighbors already did it."

"You live here?"

"Yes. I thought you already knew."

The last time she'd seen the hairdresser, they were visiting her at work.

"Did you know the men in 17B?"

Kim shrugged. "Honestly, I didn't have any interest in getting to know those two better. They didn't seem to want to make friends either, never talked to anyone."

"Did you ever see them with someone else, a woman?"

"Not sure any woman would go in there freely...no. Sorry I can't help you."

"No problem. Take care and call me if you think of anything."

"Sure thing," Kim promised.

"What are you thinking?" Derek asked when they were in the stairwell—the only elevator in this building didn't inspire trust, and after having to make minute adjustments to her wedding dress, Jordan had sworn to make some changes. Life with Ellie had spoiled her—not that she could blame Ellie for it but curling up next to her in the morning was so much more tempting than a run or the gym.

Of course, that wasn't the kind of thoughts Derek had asked for.

"Could be coincidence. In any case, this is Chucky's turf, so he should be of some help here."

"Let's hope so."

Chucky Mulveney led them into *Rigley's* through the back. "I'd like it better if you didn't come to see me in plain daylight," he complained. "It's bad for my reputation."

"There I thought you'd value your freedom more than your reputation."

Mulveney had been busted for illegal gambling and possession before, but he had cut a deal and agreed to be their eyes and ears in the area for a lesser sentence. Running *Rigley's* now, he was back on his feet in more than one way. Despite his whining Jordan thought that he was quite enjoying this role.

"All right, what do you want?"

"We just came from the apartment building across the street. Two guys shot in the head, looks like a pro job."

"Ryan Lemont would be the guy with the connections to pull that off, but you busted him. Besides, I don't think he'd like it around here. Guy's a bit of a snob, no?"

"That's all you have?" Derek asked, sounding impatient.

"What did you think I could tell you?"

"Hm...Someone in your situation might watch his neighbors a little more closely," Jordan suggested.

"Right, and if you watch your neighbors too closely, you might get killed. You probably know more about what's going on in that building than I do, but it's small stuff. Back in the days of Ryder, something like this might have happened, but you remember he came from out of town as well. There are a few big events coming up, so I imagine lots of folks who are not from around here, are doing business."

"We'll look into that."

"And I'm sure you'll be back," Mulveney concluded. "I'll see if I can talk to a few people, but don't expect too much."

"Do we ever?"

The sarcasm was lost on him, so Jordan decided not to push the issue. "Thanks. See you around."

"Sure. Not too often, would be great."

It came to no surprise that Ted Hart was a false ID. Running the prints of both men, they came up with the names of Bill Oswald and Frank Dinkins. Both of them had served time, the charges varied, but assault was a returning pattern. Interestingly enough, there was no entry in the past five years—they had either kept their heads down or managed not to get caught. However, the men had served their sentences in prisons two states apart, at different times. It was still anyone's guess as to how—and why—they had rented the apartment four weeks ago.

Before catching up with Torres, Jordan took a moment to stop by Ellie's desk. Ellie looked intensely focused on the file in front of her.

"Hey, Mrs. Carpenter."

Ellie swiveled her chair around, a smile lighting up her face.

"Hello there, Mrs. Harding."

At her own desk, Maria was rolling her eyes. "You are so adorable, it's quite painful."

"Sorry?" Jordan turned back to Ellie. "How's it going?"

"Well, things started out okay, but now I'm waiting for the ME, and my suspect's lawyer, while my partner is AWOL as usual these days. But when he's around, he sweeps in and takes the credit. And he's going way too fast again."

Jordan took a seat across from her. "You should talk to the lieutenant. This is not okay. He was supposed to give you advice when needed."

Truth be told, Ellie was probably doing a better job by herself. If she could tough it out until Waters' retirement in a few weeks, she would likely be partnered with Doss, and it would be smooth sailing from there. But they still had some time to go, and if Waters was sabotaging her, Carroll needed to know.

"I'm sure the lieutenant has an idea of what's going on, and he's not happy about it either. Okay. Here comes Ms. Gilbert's attorney." She got to her feet to greet him.

"Hey, Jimmy," Jordan said, surprised at the sight. "I didn't know you were back haunting the town."

Public defender James McKenzie was sharp and passionate, and not too popular with the prosecutors. Jordan remembered him from when she was still in uniform, and her early days as a detective.

"And you never left, I see. Why don't we catch up later? I'm here to see Detective Harding."

"Go easy. She's my wife." Ellie shot her a quizzical look, but McKenzie laughed. "Is that so? You're full of surprises, Carpenter. Nice to see you again. Detective?"

"Yes. Please follow me," Ellie said, obviously still trying to make sense of the scene.

Jordan was still musing about the unexpected encounter when she joined Nina Torres in the briefing room.

Nina had already set up a board, placing a question mark over the photograph of the closet. Jordan's stomach churned as she remembered the smell.

"It looks like these guys could have been involved in all sorts of criminal activity," she remarked. "But it might not be local at all. Maybe they were hiding out, and whoever they were hiding from, found them anyway."

"It's possible." Torres didn't sound convinced.

"One of our sources thinks that hit might have come from out of town."

"What do you think?"

"It's a possibility. We sent many folks associated with Ryder and Lemont to prison over the years. Those who were on the fringe...can't imagine them hiring a hit man, let alone to kill someone who just moved into town."

"Pre-emptive strike? How reliable is your source?"

Jordan almost winced. The association with Mulveney was a new one, and at this point, still a bit shaky. She assumed he'd do the bare minimum that would keep him out of jail.

"He's...motivated. I'm also interested in the contents of that closet. Did they come to town to kidnap someone?"

"Again, perhaps they weren't on the run from anyone, but trying to establish themselves. Whatever they did, they were extremely careful. Once they served their time, they simply vanished. Next and last sign of life, Ted Hart's credit card."

"I'm still trying to figure out what's the FBI's interest in this." Jordan was uncomfortably reminded of the time explosives dealers had tried to make a deal in town. Fortunately, the bomber had worked alone, and they could contain his ambitions before they led to a catastrophe. "With the sports event coming up, were you thinking...terrorism? Do you have any concrete hints? In that case, don't you think we should know?"

The kidnapping case could be a distraction. Ellie's abductor had moved on to bigger plans when she got away from him. She didn't want to think about this right now, especially with Nina studying her curiously.

"No, that's not it," Nina said. "You were wondering what connects these men, when apparently, they never met before they moved into this apartment? Both were hanging with an especially ugly crowd. Sex crimes has a file on both of them. Violent movies on the dark net, involving underage girls."

In a heartbeat, the possibilities had become so much worse.

"I wish there was some sort of silver lining, and whoever they locked into that closet, got away, but it's not likely, is it? The people who killed Oswald and Dinkins probably took them. I hate this day already."

"Let's not jump to conclusions. Perhaps we can find out who they are. Go from there."

"How is this related...?" Jordan gave herself the answer before Nina could. "You're thinking about human trafficking. "That is why you were on the scene right away. You were already on those guys."

"Dr. Roberts told me not to underestimate you. Not that I intended to. It's true, we were suspecting both of them, but unfortunately, they got themselves killed before we could get to them. They are mid-level at best. We still need to find the people they were answering to, and as a special challenge, who killed them, so hopefully, we can contain what will be going on behind the scenes of the game."

"There's no question in any of that, so you're sure something will be going on either way. That's depressing."

"We'll be prepared," Nina said.

⁂

"Detective Harding, it's a pleasure to meet you. And please, don't mind the shenanigans. I was happy to see a familiar face. Someone in my profession isn't too well liked around here, as you can imagine."

"It's fine," Ellie told him. "What can I do for you?"

"As you know, I represent Brandi Gilbert, and I was wondering about the circumstances of her arrest. Some things don't add up in here."

*Don't I know it...*She couldn't say it out loud, but silently, Ellie agreed with McKenzie.

"The bodyguard, Mr. Owens, said that he walked in on her standing over Robertson with the gun in her hand. Ms. Gilbert admitted to shooting him. I'm afraid we had no choice."

"And she supposedly brought the gun with her?"

"It wasn't Mr. Robertson's. It's unregistered."

"See, that's strange. There is no way Ms. Gilbert could have brought the gun with her. She simply had no opportunity. Robertson wasn't worth anything to her pimp if he was dead. So, killing him for the money, with that mystery gun, it makes your case quite thin, even if she said she did it."

"My colleague established motive...Robertson had a lot of money with him."

"And she would have done what with it? Someone was standing by outside waiting for her. You'd think they'd let her keep it?"

"I think..." Ellie paused, knowing she could either stick to Waters' line, or walk down a potentially dangerous path. But Waters had rushed proceedings, just to get back at her, or so it seemed. She didn't understand his motives, but whatever was behind his actions, they could potentially tarnish her career as well, and the whole department. "Even if she pulled the trigger, I don't see her as a cold-blooded killer. Something happened in that apartment that we don't yet know about."

"Hallelujah. I knew Carpenter wouldn't marry a fool," he said. "You were the first investigator to talk to her. What was your impression?"

"She seemed afraid—of everyone there, Mr. Owens, the police. Traumatized. I was wondering if a psychiatrist should see her."

"Bravo. We have an understanding here. Look, she told me that Mr. Robertson always treated her decently, which, I think we both know, doesn't say much in this context. She's disturbed and afraid. Perhaps we can both agree here that Ms. Gilbert probably hasn't told us the whole truth yet, because public defenders and the police haven't done much to earn her trust in the past. How about we try to make a change here?"

"I'm with you on that, though we can't ignore the fact that a person is dead."

"I don't intend to, but I'm sure you agree that context matters."

"I do," Ellie confirmed. "I'd definitely like to find out more about the people who kept sending her to Robertson's. I'll see her before the hearing tomorrow."

"And I'll get the psychiatrist involved. Thank you, Detective Harding. This has been most enlightening."

Ellie thought the same, even if it was probably only a matter of time before she'd be in hot water with her partner. She straightened her shoulders. So be it. In the past, Lieutenant Carroll had always seen her point—this would be no exception.

Chances were Waters wouldn't even find out until the next day.

Chapter Three

I t looked like she'd be lucky. Waters didn't talk much for the rest of the day, but he didn't mention her meeting with McKenzie. Ellie couldn't wait to find Jordan and go home.

That would have to wait, she realized when she returned to her desk and saw Officer Potts standing next to it with a woman who seemed to be in her late thirties.

"This is Ms. Morgan. She'd like to talk to you."

"Thanks, Sam. Hi. I'm Detective Harding." After being in awe for some time, the words now came over her lips easily. "How can I help you?"

"I'm Natalie Morgan. If I could have a moment of your time?"

"Sure. Please, sit."

"Thank you." The woman seemed a bit nervous, but nothing that indicated an immediate emergency. "The reason I come to you is...my mother died recently."

"I'm sorry for your loss." Did she suspect foul play?

"Thank you. I know what you must be thinking but...that's not the reason I'm here. This is hard...It turns out Mom kept some pretty big secrets from me. From everyone she cared about, actually."

Ellie was intrigued but still wondering about Morgan's reasons for seeking out the police. For seeking out Ellie, specifically. Had she, or had she simply asked to talk to an investigator?

"You know that this is the Homicide unit."

"Yes, I do. Okay. There's no way around this, but I am so glad we finally meet." Natalie took a picture out of her purse and handed it to Ellie. "She always told me she didn't know who my father was. The way she explained it to me, I made my peace. I was okay with it, but it seems that people feel a need to clear things up towards the end. So, she told me the truth."

Ellie could feel her jaw drop when she looked at the picture. She'd never seen the auburn-haired woman, Natalie's mother, before, but she knew the man who had an arm around her waist, both of them beaming. The scenery looked like they were on a beach somewhere. That man was Patrick Harding. Her father.

"This is impossible." She hoped that if she said it out loud, it had to be true. There was no way in hell he had cheated on her mother...was there?

"I understand this is a shock," Natalie said softly. "I wasn't sure either if I wanted to hear the story, but please, let me explain. It's not as bad as you think. They were together a short time, had fun, lost touch for a while. The next time they talked, Patrick told her he was happy and in love, about to get married."

"Wow."

"Mom had really loved him as a friend, and she didn't want him to change plans out of obligation. I don't blame her for anything. Growing up...it was an adventure. I wouldn't want to miss that for anything. I won't lie, I hoped I'd be able to meet my father, but then I learned about the accident..." She wiped a hand over her eyes. "You have lost so much, too. I know I'm a stranger to you, but I guess I was hoping I could get to know you. Mom and I, we made a lot of friends all over the world, but my grandparents are deceased as well, and you're the only family I have left."

Something about that statement hit Ellie hard, and she hadn't even recovered from the whiplash learning about the other relationship her father had had. It wasn't like she'd imagined neither of her parents had dated anyone else before they got married. She just hadn't thought about it at all.

"I understand you need time. It took me a while to work up my courage to come here. I visited the grave...I hope you don't mind I've been leaving flowers."

"That's okay, of course. I'd been wondering about that."

"Anyway, I felt like I couldn't keep this to myself any longer. This is my number." She snatched a pen and some sticky notes from Ellie's desk and jotted down the numbers. "I hope you'll call me when you're ready. Thank you for seeing me."

She got to her feet. Ellie was slow to react, but she finally did. "Please, wait, Ms...Natalie. How about now? I mean, if you don't have any plans. Would you like to have dinner with me and my wife?"

She had gotten used to the term detective. This new aspect of her reality never failed to fill her with excitement.

Natalie turned to her with a surprised smile. "Are you sure?"

"Absolutely. I was about to leave, and I could call her...but here she is." Jordan had just come inside, heading straight for Ellie's desk.

"You're ready to go?"

"Yes. And I have a surprise for you. Meet Natalie—my sister."

In the biological sense, Natalie Morgan was the closest thing she had to family, too. Ellie had once promised herself to never waste any chances, and this situation definitely qualified.

25

Jordan was happy for Ellie. These days, she was just plain happy, and grateful that this day had taken a turn for the better, even if she couldn't help thinking it was a little strange. Why wait for weeks to come see Ellie? Then again, it had taken her own mother two decades to find the courage to talk to her. She was hardly one to judge, and Natalie seemed pleasant. In any case, she didn't seem to have any problem with the fact that her half-sister was married to a woman. Jordan would give her credit for that.

"So, what do you do?" she asked, when they had sat down at the restaurant with a first glass of wine, the sharp edges of first surprise mellowing.

"I'm afraid it's not nearly as exciting as your job. Wow. You deal with really dangerous individuals. I work in an office. It's safe and boring, and that totally works for me."

"Believe me, some days the greatest danger I'm in is from a paper cut."

Not that today had been dangerous in any sense of the word, but if Nina's predictions were true, they could be kicking a hornet's nest with this investigation. She would have liked to see how Ellie's day had gone, especially since she'd overheard Waters grumbling about the case, but that would have to wait.

"Forgive me if I don't believe that. You put away some high-profile criminals." Natalie smiled self-consciously. "I'll admit when I learned that Ellie's with the police, I did some homework. You saved a woman from a burning car."

She appeared to know a lot about Ellie already. Ellie, on the other hand, still seemed too stunned to ask a lot of questions. Jordan could think of some, but it wasn't her place.

"How did you find me?" Ellie asked.

"The Internet was a great help. With what Mom gave me, I could do some research, and so I learned about the accident, and that you existed. Then, your name came up a time or two in the paper, and so I knew where to look."

It sounded legit enough so far.

"I didn't want to act like a stalker, but I wanted to be sure I knew at least a little bit about what I was going to walk into. This is so much better than I hoped. I think Mom would be very happy. I'm sorry. It's just amazing."

Only a day after they'd returned from their honeymoon, it truly was.

"Would you like to come to our house for a coffee?" Ellie asked.

Jordan asked herself if it was time to put on the brakes sometime soon. She didn't want her to be disappointed.

Natalie Morgan smiled. "I'd love to," she said.

⁂

"Oh my God, it's late! I'm so sorry," Natalie exclaimed when she looked at her watch. "Way to make a first impression. I hope I can call you again sometime?"

"Please. I'd love that," Ellie said, getting up to see her out. She, too, was amazed how time had seemed to slip away as they talked over coffee. For some reason, the situation wasn't as painfully awkward as it could have been. They both had questions some of which the other one could answer. Ellie was grateful to realize her emotions had changed, softened over time—she could talk about her parents with love and pride rather than the all-encompassing pain she'd felt for years.

Thanks to Jordan, and Madeline, a friend of Meredith and Patrick's she had reconnected with recently—this chance encounter made a difference as well. She had a sister.

"Excuse me," she said, laughing, while they were waiting for Natalie's cab. "This is still surreal to me."

"I understand. But good, I hope."

"Yes. I am happy now, but for a long time, I felt very alone. Not just lonely, but like no one would understand me. I'd definitely like to keep in touch."

"Great. Why don't we have lunch sometime this week? Just the two of us, if you can get away from work for a bit?"

"I'm sure I can do that sometime. Where's your office again?"

"In the Mason tower. It's not that far from the station, and it has some really great restaurants."

"Sounds good."

The driver arrived, parking on the curb. Ellie almost stepped forward to hug Natalie, remembering at the last moment that she'd only met her a few hours ago. That was the reason, right? It was only normal. She watched as Natalie waved and got into the backseat, then she turned back for the house. What a crazy day it had been. And tomorrow would be busy as hell too. She needed to squeeze in meeting Brandi Gilbert before her hearing. Before Waters got wind that she'd shared some opinions with the public defender. Ellie remembered that she meant to ask Jordan about him. That seemed like forever ago.

In the living room, Jordan was almost asleep, but she opened her arms as Ellie curled up next to her on the couch.

"This is really tempting, but we should go to bed. Early start tomorrow."

"You and me both." Jordan sighed but made no attempt to move.

Wife, Ellie thought, unable to hold back the smile. Ellie loved everything about being married. They had been living together for a while now, so nothing specific had actually changed, but it was hard to ignore the milestone it presented, an added depth to their commitment.

For the first time in her life, she felt like she had arrived somewhere, in a place where it was okay to remain without constantly seeking out the next challenge. In her job. In her relationship. Now, the appearance of a family member she hadn't known about. The timing might be odd, but odd things happened in life. This was one to be grateful for. She had many blessings to count—but getting up early in the morning after a lack of sleep wasn't one of them.

"Come on. I really need some horizontal time."

"Promises, promises," Jordan murmured, but she let herself be led into the main suite.

⌁

"Do you think I went too fast?" Ellie asked when they were having breakfast the next morning. "In the moment, it seemed the right thing to do. Now I wonder if I was a little too intense."

"You can be pretty intense, and I love that about you." Jordan who stood by the coffeemaker, bend to kiss her neck softly. "I think she was okay. She stayed until after midnight, after all."

As if on cue, Ellie yawned. "This is still so weird, out of the blue. I have a sister. I'm baffled, I'm happy, and I feel a little guilty for thinking I should maybe run a background check on her."

"Well, you know we're not supposed to use these sources for personal purposes...I'm with you on that. On the other hand...It never hurts to be prepared."

"That's not paranoid, is it?"

Jordan sat across from her. "Maybe a little. But for the world we live in, it's justified. Just basics, to make sure she is who she says she is. I can take care of that."

The quick agreement told Ellie that Jordan had been thinking about it. So, it wasn't just her. And she didn't mean to doubt Natalie's story or discredit a dead woman. She simply didn't want anything to mar this unexpected, great experience.

"That would be great. Thank you. I have to go to the morgue, deal with my partner, and squeeze in a meeting sometime before the afternoon, and by the way, I completely forgot to ask you about McKenzie."

"Hang on a second. Is Waters still giving you trouble?"

Ellie shrugged. "Not more than the usual. Don't worry about it. He'll be gone in a few weeks."

"Still, if it gets too much, talk to Carroll. He's going to listen."

"I know. Now, about you and James..."

Jordan shook her head, laughing. "Well, you met him. Back in the days, we were the only openly gay people we knew around here, so we connected over that."

"You trust his judgment?"

"Absolutely, and not because he's gay. He goes for very specific cases."

"Yeah, like mine...Is there really a good reason for shooting someone five times?" Ellie gave herself the answer. "Perhaps that's not the right question, or the question I should ask. Someone's dead, and it's my job to find who did it, and prove it. All else is out of my hands."

"Waters said you made an arrest?"

"Yeah, we did. I think she did it. She confessed, and all evidence points to that...well, that's where McKenzie comes in. He's interested in the context, and frankly, I am too."

"Yeah, he's big on that. Are you going to call Natalie?"

"I was going to give her a couple of days."

"That's probably a good idea."

Chapter Four

S he knew Ellie was going to talk to the medical examiner this morning, so Jordan wasn't surprised when she and Nina ran into her in front of the double doors. They had barely said hello when Dr. Adams stepped out.

"Agent Torres, Detective Carpenter, Detective Harding," Dr. Adams greeted them.

"I guess you're all here for the same reason, but I'm afraid one of you will have to wait."

"I just need a second, please," Ellie started. "Do you have anything new for me regarding Mr. Robertson?"

"She's my favorite, always says please and thank you," Dr. Adams commented dryly. "However, someone was in a hurry regarding the guys in 17B."

"Sorry about that," Torres said in a pleasant tone. "This was urgent."

"But Robertson was supposed to be first..."

Jordan didn't envy Ellie. With no news from the ME, she might be in for an uncomfortable conversation with her partner this morning. However, she could see Nina's point. If the murders of Dinkins and Oswald were linked to organized crime, and there might be a witness out there, this had to take priority.

"Sorry, Harding. The lady from the FBI says it's urgent, those are the bodies I have to take care of first. Come back later?"

Ellie's expression clearly showed her disappointment, but she didn't try to argue. "I guess I will. Thanks anyway. I'll see you."

Jordan and Nina followed Dr. Adams into her office. "Now, don't get your hopes up too high either. Most of what I found is what you'd expect. One shot to the head each, in quick succession. There were no defensive wounds, no sign that they tried to run away."

"So, the person who killed them must have been a professional—at the very least, well-trained. Anything else? Those guys were so under the radar, they were practically ghosts."

"Well, I can tell you they had Chinese food for their last meal. Some time between eight and ten last night, time of death soon after."

The food containers in the closet came from a nearby restaurant chain. It had been closed yesterday, but today, they hoped to talk to some employees.

"That's good. Someone might have seen them."

They could only hope that the employees, and possibly clientele of the restaurant were more helpful than the men's neighbors. She might have to introduce Nina to Chucky as well.

"Any drugs in their system?" Nina asked, making Jordan wonder if she had a theory.

"Nope, just some beer."

That would probably match the empty bottles in the trash.

"Blood stains on the mattress didn't match either of them, to no surprise."

"Yeah, I imagined that. Thanks, Doc."

They got lucky not much later—the print recognition software showed them the record of a young woman once arrested for a DUI, four years ago. Since she was eighteen at the time, the record hadn't been sealed. Isabel Combs had been reported missing only a few months later, before her nineteenth birthday.

She had vanished after spending an afternoon at the local mall with two friends.

A quick call to the restaurant confirmed that the employees working the night of the murder would come in later in the afternoon. They'd meet them there—enough time to dig deeper into Isabel Combs' disappearance.

Her photo was going around in the media once more.

⁕

Detective Waters was not amused when Ellie told him about her experience at the morgue.

"Who's running this department anyway?" he snapped. "You can't just let things like that slide."

"I'm sorry, but what was I supposed to do? Agent Torres had already asked…"

"Agent Torres doesn't work here, and Adams knows that. What's her problem?"

"Harding, Waters, could you please come into my office for a moment?" the lieutenant called.

Ellie hoped it wouldn't take too long. She had to see Brandi Gilbert before she went before the judge.

"I want to make sure you're on the same page here."

"This is impossible. Gilbert will see the judge today. It would help to deal with any unforeseen surprises if we had some results at least."

"I agree, but Special Agent Torres asked for a courtesy, and there's a lot at stake. Why would you think there could be unforeseen surprises with your case? You have a confession, the murder weapon, a witness—shouldn't be a problem, should it? Harding, you don't look convinced," Carroll commented.

Ellie straightened in her chair. "I have no doubts, sir."

"Good. That's all."

It looked like she would have enough time to steal away for a meeting with McKenzie and Gilbert.

⁂

"Why are you here? I thought you already have everything you need. I'm in here." She raised her shackled wrists. "Is that not enough?"

Compared to the last time she'd seen her, Brandi Gilbert looked surprisingly composed, Ellie thought. It didn't sound like she was much cooperative, but at least she had agreed to this meeting with Ellie and McKenzie. Ellie would make the most of it.

"I have a few more questions." That my colleague neglected to ask. "How many times have you been to Mr. Robertson's apartment?"

"Three times. Maybe four."

"Please, try to be as precise as possible."

"Okay, four. What difference does it make? You're not going to ask me why I was there?"

"He paid you?" Ellie asked, unfazed by the challenging tone.

"Girl, are you new or what? He paid the money upfront, in Hank's account. They all do. Otherwise, I wouldn't get near that house."

"Hank. Can you tell me his last name?"

"Why don't you try to figure it out?"

"Ms. Gilbert," McKenzie warned. "The detective is here to help."

She snorted. "That would be a first."

"You know what's going to happen when you walk into the courtroom later? The judge will know this about you—you shot a man five times. It would help if you could tell us why."

"Really? Help who? There's no life for me anywhere."

"What happened that night? You didn't decide to shoot him, just like that?" She was probably far beyond things that she could and should say to the woman without jeopardizing her case, but Ellie was getting frustrated with her changing attitude. She kept her tone low, reminding herself that she only knew a fraction of what the woman had been through. "You asked me if I had arrested Mr. Owens. What did you think I arrested him for?"

"I don't know. I wasn't thinking clearly."

"I believe that. Maybe you weren't thinking clearly when you pulled that trigger either? This wasn't Mr. Robertson's gun. Who gave it to you, if it wasn't yours?"

"I don't know. I don't remember!"

Ellie cast a look at McKenzie.

"I had a psychiatrist talk to Ms. Gilbert earlier this morning," he explained. "There are too many unexplained questions right now, especially regarding Mr. Owens, who is the only witness. Perhaps you could warn your partner and the A.D.A. that the case is thin."

"I'd like to talk to Mr. McKenzie alone for a moment," Ellie said.

"That's okay, I think we're done here," McKenzie told his client. "Ms. Gilbert, I'll see you later, and remember everything I told you."

"Yeah, right. I have nothing else to do."

Ellie shook her head when they were outside the room.

"I have to admit, I didn't expect that. It's like talking to a different person."

"Except one thing that remains the same."

"She's still terrified, I get that."

"It seems like every once in a while the gravity of what happened, and the consequences, sink in, then there's something else that scares her more. Your instincts were right on the money regarding the psychiatrist. The gaps in her memory indicate trauma, either from committing the murder, or witnessing it, but as long as we don't know for sure, I think this woman needs help more than she needs prison."

"I'll be back later," Ellie said, doubts plaguing her. Either way, she was going to face consequences as well. On her way back to town, she called Darla Pierson, Jordan's former CI, at work. It wasn't more than a hunch at this point, but she was the only one Ellie knew that might help her.

"I swear I'm not going to bother you too long. I just have one question. I have this woman here who says she worked for a Hank, but she didn't give me a last name. It's probably foolish to think that..."

"Wow. Hank. I can't say for sure it's the same guy, but it would be a huge coincidence, right? I never met him in person. He does escort for rich folks who are in town for business. From what I heard, he's brutal. I can try to find out more..."

Ellie already felt bad. "You have another job that I'm keeping you from. I'm sorry, forget about it, okay?"

"Are you sure? In any case, be careful. He's very elusive, and vengeful with everyone who tries to get in his way." So far, nothing she hadn't seen before. Darla continued, "He runs things out of Webster, rarely comes to town himself. He doesn't have to. His guys are extremely loyal. Oh, and here comes my boss. See you, Ellie."

"Yeah. Thanks."

She had barely made it inside the building when Waters found her, enraged.

"What the hell were you thinking?"

Okay, now was apparently the moment. Somehow, Ellie understood that stalling wouldn't help her.

"The public defender, McKenzie, asked to see me first, and he had some compelling arguments why the case isn't that cut and dried. Mr. Owens for example..."

"Oh please, Harding, let's not go down that rabbit hole again."

"Why not? I was right about—"

"We closed the Goddamn case, handed Esposito everything she needed, now McKenzie is going to introduce a motion for dismissal. You know what that means, Harding?" He didn't wait for an answer. "You screwed up, badly. I'm going to ask the lieutenant to take you off the case. Hell, perhaps it would do you some good to direct traffic for a while."

"What is wrong with you?" Ellie never wanted to have that conversation, at work, especially not with him. If she was honest, there had always been the chance for it to happen, but she'd hoped it wouldn't be necessary before his last day. "I have the name of a pimp who works with high profile clients. There might or might not be a connection to Owens, but in any case, he didn't see her shoot Robertson. She has gaps in her memory. Why do you think it's acceptable that we make a mistake here?"

He shook his head. "Get off your high horse. Gilbert confessed, now she wants to plead not guilty. If this case falls apart, it's your fault, no one else's."

"I did nothing wrong."

"Don't be surprised if IA wants to look into this. Makes a person wonder which side you are on." He stalked away, leaving Ellie standing.

"Asshole," she muttered under her breath. Not quietly enough, apparently, because he spun around.

"What did you say?"

"Nothing."

This time, Ellie was the one to walk away.

Chapter Five

I sabel Combs' parents still lived on the outskirts of town. Mrs. Combs opened the door to them, faltering at seeing police on their doorstep again.

"After all this time—that can only mean one thing, right?" She started crying.

"Mrs. Combs, please, can we come inside for a moment?" Torres asked. Throwing a glance over her shoulder, Jordan could detect movement behind more than one window in neighbors' houses. They were wondering too.

"We wanted to warn you that Isabel's picture will be on the evening news. We don't know where she is—yet—but there's new evidence."

"Is she alive?" Mrs. Combs asked incredulously. "Is my baby alive?"

"We don't know." Jordan hated having to repeat it. "We found proof that she's been in an apartment downtown until recently."

"What does that mean? Someone held her there? Where are they now? What are you doing to find them?"

Jordan exchanged a look with Nina, who said, "The men who rented the apartment, are dead. We are doing everything we can to find Isabel. Her picture will be shared on the TV stations' social media, and officers are on the lookout for her."

Mrs. Combs looked like this was far too much, overwhelming information for her.

"When is your husband coming home?" she asked.

"He should be on his way here. God, what did they do to her?"

"We shouldn't jump to any conclusions," Jordan said, though she had to admit it was hard not to. She hoped that Isabel, wherever she was, had gotten away from her captors rather than gotten caught up in something even worse.

⚜

The employees of the Chinese restaurant, a man and a woman, confirmed that Dinkins and Oswald had bought takeout on the night of the murders, and that they had frequented the restaurant, sometimes having their meals there.

While Isabel Combs was locked in the closet? Jordan wondered. Neither of them had seen or remembered her.

The smell of food was almost overwhelming. There had been no lunch break earlier as they dug into Combs' story, and she was glad they could leave the restaurant soon after. Earlier, they had gotten a call from the lab that confirmed the presence of a fourth print, only partial, too smudged to be worth something for them. They were still working on evidence from the scene. The fourth person could be the killer.

"Four years. That's a long time to resurface. Why here and now, why with those people?"

"If we knew that, things would be a lot easier," Nina said. "I don't think we're going to find out tonight. Say, could you recommend a decent place for a drink and some bar food?"

"Sure. You want to check in and go after? I'm starving."

"Sounds great."

Torres was driving, so Jordan used the time to text Ellie and Derek to direct them to the *Night Shift*. Kate, Ellie's best friend and Derek's girlfriend, might join them too.

Neither Ellie nor Derek was at the station, but they had both checked in and confirmed they'd meet them at the bar.

When they walked through the doors of the *Night Shift*, both were there, sitting at a table in the corner. Ellie was holding her head in her hands. Derek looked sympathetic.

"Hey guys. Agent Torres was looking for a place to eat, so I told her about this one...is everything okay?"

Ellie cast a quick look at Torres, and then mumbled, "Yes, sure. Hi. Sorry about earlier."

"No problem," Torres returned.

A rather awkward pause ensued. "All right. Let's get drinks? Ellie, would you come with me?" Jordan waited until everyone had made their choice, and the two of them were out of earshot. "Okay, what's going on?"

"McKenzie introduced a motion for dismissal, based on the conversations we had."

"Ouch. Did the judge go for it?"

"No. There was blood on the woman's shirt, and residue on her hands. She doesn't remember...I think there's some prolonged trauma at work, and the psychiatrist said the same. Judge didn't go for that either. I think Waters is happy, but he bad-mouthed me to the lieutenant first."

"Wow. I'm sorry. That's not something you should tough out until he's gone. What did Carroll say?"

"Not much. He tried to be diplomatic. What I'm hearing between the lines is, he'll be glad once Waters retires, too. He is the senior detective, and I should consult with him, but how am I supposed to do that when he's either dismissing me, or not present at all? How is that going to teach me anything?"

"You are absolutely right. Don't let this go. Ask to talk to Carroll, ask to be partnered with someone else. I could—"

"No," was Ellie's categorical answer.

"Okay, fine. I'm sure Doss would love to work with you."

"She loves her freedom, but yes, I'd so prefer her…You know what I mean," Ellie added after realizing her words were open to different interpretations.

"Yes, I know what you mean," Jordan assured her, glad Ellie was able to have a sense of humor about the situation. She didn't think Waters could truly harm Ellie's career, but he had become a nuisance. "And I'm really sorry about your day. I'll make it up to you later, I promise."

Ellie smiled. "I'll take you up on that—even though it wasn't your fault, and it wasn't even all bad. So, it's going well with Torres?"

"So far, so good. I have a bad feeling about the case, like it's one of those that could be growing heads. If we could at least find the missing woman…"

"Yeah. I hope you can."

Their drinks finally arrived, and they went back to the table where Derek and Nina were engaged in what looked like a pleasant conversation.

Jordan wasn't too happy with what Ellie had revealed regarding Waters. While she knew Ellie could handle herself, she would keep an eye on the situation. Everything else seemed to be moving forward. As they sat back down at the table, it crossed her mind that there were some striking similarities between hers and Ellie's case, both involving women in desperate situations that might or might not have taken justice into their own hands.

Coincidence?

She caught Nina's curious glance, wondering what the reason was, until she picked up her glass and realized it was her wedding ring that had caught the agent's attention.

"I guess we should try to get something to eat," she said. "I promised Agent Torres some decent food."

Ellie called Natalie first thing in the morning, and they made a date for lunch at a bistro in the Mason tower. Part of her wondered about what could have been if they had met as children, but she never spent a lot of time on hypothetical questions. Natalie's mom had probably sought to keep her from disappointment in a complicated situation. Not that Ellie could ever imagine her father not taking responsibility for his own child—but if he had known, that might have set a series of even more complicated events into motion.

No, Natalie had found her at the right time, when she was truly content and at home in her life. Something she would have loved to share with her parents, but now she got to share it with a sibling she didn't know existed.

Truth be told those thoughts were also helpful distracting her from the work situation, and Jordan's suggestion. Could she really have that talk with Carroll? Should she? Jordan had been around longer than she had, but then again, she also had years of successful work to show for. Ellie had joined the unit only recently, and she was supposed to learn from a more experienced colleague. She was supposed to fit into the team. If she couldn't make it work, would that say more about her than it did about Waters?

Waters wasn't there when she arrived. This was perhaps a good idea to get a quick coffee before he yelled at her again.

Everything would be easier if she got to work with Doss. She would have liked to look into Hank some more. Together, they could perhaps even come up with a strategy to get to him directly, except that her partner wasn't interested, and she either had to go through him or wait it out. A lot could happen in a few weeks.

Lieutenant Carroll wasn't in his office. Ellie decided to lay low until she could talk to him.

❧

Nina Torres, aside from getting Dr. Adams to prioritize their case, kept a pretty low profile, compared to Bethany, anyway. They worked on tracing the last steps of Dinkins and Oswald while trying everything possible to find Isabel Combs—as to this moment, with no success. This could mean several things. She might not want to be found, a reasonable aim considering what her experiences likely were. The other explanation was that she, too, was dead.

Jordan wasn't ready to accept that interpretation yet, and neither was Nina. They decided to go back to the area while a uniformed officer was answering calls to the hotline.

As usual, there were many calls to filter through—nothing helpful so far.

"Could you wait a second?" Jordan asked when they walked past Lieutenant Carroll in the hallway. This was probably a bad idea, but she had reached the end of her patience. She was well aware that Ellie needed to be careful, being the last detective to have been hired into the unit. It was true that she still had things to learn, but if Waters was determined to make everyone miserable during his last weeks, nothing much would come out of it.

"Sure." Nina leaned against the wall as Jordan hurried after her supervisor.

"Sir. Do you have a minute?"

"I hope you have something new about Ms. Combs?"

"I'm sorry, not yet. This won't take long though. I was wondering if you had any plans to partner Ellie with Detective Doss...and if this could happen sooner rather than later. I think it would help the case."

"You think so, Detective?"

She detected the slightest hint of impatience, trying not to cringe.

"Did Harding put you up to this?"

"No. Of course not. She would never." Damn. Ellie would not be happy about this. Perhaps she had overestimated how aware Carroll was of the recent dynamics?

"I think that's something we can agree on. If changes are necessary, we will make them. Is that all?"

It wasn't very satisfying, but she wasn't going to push her luck.

"Yes, sir. Thanks."

"Any problems I should know about?" Torres asked when they were in the car. She was driving, her hands relaxed on the steering wheel.

"Not really."

"All right then. Thanks for letting me come yesterday. It's a nice place."

"Yeah." She wasn't much in the mood for small talk either. Jordan had gotten up with a headache and an overall tension that could be a hint something was about to happen. Sometimes, it was just there to annoy her. At least Ellie would meet with Natalie again, which reminded her of the background check she had promised. She'd have to be less obvious about it than with her earlier conversation with the lieutenant.

Across the street from the Chinese restaurant the men had frequented was a coffee shop. There weren't many students with laptops in this area, but the few patrons looked young, a girl by the window shivering in a big sweater, even though it wasn't all that cold. Following a hunch, she went inside. Nina went with her, waiting as Jordan showed Combs' picture to the woman behind the counter.

"No, I'm sorry. I've never seen her."

"What about these gentlemen?"

The waitress barely flinched at the photographs, even though it was obvious that both men were dead. The people in this neighborhood, including Kim Geller and Chucky Mulveney, didn't flinch easily.

She pointed to Dinkins' picture. "He was here a few times, with a girl. A different one each time. One time, he chatted up one of the customers. I remember because I asked her if she was okay. She said yes."

"Different girls, but not Isabel?"

"That's what I said. Excuse me?" she added when a customer came in.

Jordan waited until he had ordered. "When does your shift end?"

"Someone's coming in to take over at six, why?"

"I'd like you to come in later and look at some pictures. Perhaps you'll recognize those girls."

"Look, they seemed legal. There was nothing I could do..."

"Just please come by, Ms...Lewis. We'll be waiting for you."

Nina was suspiciously silent when they walked back to the car.

"You don't agree that she should come in?" Jordan asked.

"No, it's a good idea," she said. "It's just depressing, right? It happens right before their eyes, and no one even thinks of doing anything."

Jordan could only agree.

Chapter Six

Natalie was wearing slacks and a sweater, with pumps. Ellie couldn't help noticing that they were dressed in a similar way, and she was secretly excited about it. She had told herself to tone it down a bit—she didn't want her only relative disappear so soon again. It wasn't easy. At least Natalie seemed as excited to see her again. She occupied a table by the window and got up to hug Ellie when she arrived.

"Hey. I'm so glad you could make it. I assume in your line of work, emergencies happen all the time."

"Some days are better than others," Ellie said, unable to keep herself from smiling. "I hope you don't mind I called you so soon. This...it's still a little unreal."

"Yeah, tell me about it. I'm happy you called. I still have so many questions."

"Me too. And there's a bunch of people I'd like you to meet." Ellie took a deep breath. "Wow, I'm sorry if that's a bit overwhelming. We can do that slowly, too."

"It's fine. I want to meet the people that are important to you."

"So, a dinner party wouldn't freak you out too much?" Ellie had meant it as a joke, but Natalie was unfazed.

"It's no problem. I already know you have a lovely wife and home, so this should be fun. Why don't we drink to that?"

"Oh, I can't. I have to go back to work."

"Just one little glass of champagne wouldn't hurt, would it?"

"I'm sorry." Ellie felt a little confused that Natalie would even argue about it. She told herself that she didn't know her new-found sister well enough to judge. "But you go right ahead, I don't mind." Wouldn't she run the risk meeting co-workers in this restaurant?

"I have the afternoon off," Natalie said, "but you're right, let's hold off the celebrating until we can both enjoy it."

To change the slightly awkward subject, Ellie began, "You said you and your mom traveled a lot. That sounds really interesting."

"Oh, it was. We made friends all over Europe and South America, but of course it's hard to keep in touch, even now with the Internet. Most of it was a long time ago. Tell me about you. Did you always want to be a cop?"

"I had been interested for a long time. After my parents died...there was a time where I couldn't bring myself to be motivated by anything. I didn't go back to my classes, and instead, I traveled, too." Another thing they had in common, though Ellie's explorations had been borne out of grief. "Not as far as you did, though. Maybe a dozen states or so. I worked here and there and tried to make sense of life."

"I understand. But you came back eventually."

"Yes. I tried out for the academy, and that was it. I always remembered the detective that came to see me that day. I remember I hated her...and then, that it takes guts to do that, so that played a role. But I got to see the detectives at work, and I knew that's where I wanted to go. I'm talking too much, right?"

"No way, I'm enjoying it. Well, not the sad part, obviously. I hate I never got the chance to meet Patrick, but I'm really happy I found you. Tell me more, please."

Ellie did, guiltily thinking about the background check she'd talked to Jordan about—and she was nearly late for work.

She waved to the waiter and when he arrived at the table, paid her lunch with her debit card while Natalie ordered another coffee.

"I really have to go now, but I'll be in touch about the party."

"I'm excited," Natalie said. "And we'll have to do this again soon."

⁘

At the station, Ellie finished up on some paperwork. Since she didn't have time for her own coffee at the restaurant, she headed to the break room between printouts. She stopped cold at the sight presenting itself to her when she opened the door. In front of the vending machine, Waters stood with Officer Potts close enough to leave no personal space. His hands were on her lower back. While her brain was still processing what she saw, Ellie realized that Sam looked distressed, the picture making sense in a disturbing way all of a sudden.

"What's going on here? Sam! Are you okay?"

Potts almost violently pulled away from the touch and fled.

"I can't believe this." Ellie shook her head, still somewhat in shock. "What the hell were you—"

"Shut the fuck up, Harding. This is none of your business."

"You just made it my business. If Sam doesn't report..."

He was in her face the next moment, angry and, she thought, pathetic. "Be very careful what you say next. You are already hanging on by a thread, constantly going off on your own. That's not going to look good for you."

"I'm not the one rushing through the process, ignoring evidence. I'll take my chances. You can't intimidate me."

"You think?" he all but spat. "You know, you all depend on that backup arriving on time."

Ellie caught a glimpse at something that, she assumed, had been simmering under the surface for a long time. He was known for mean jibes against everything and everyone he didn't like, and there was a lot Detective Waters didn't like. She knew Maria had been glad not to be working with him any longer, but he'd still mostly kept it together at the time. Lately, he'd been escalating. Assaulting a young officer and threatening a colleague was over the line. She was almost relieved. It had to end here.

"That's enough, Cliff," she said just as the door opened, and Derek Henderson walked in.

"Hey, Waters, the lieutenant wants to see you," he said curtly. "You better go now," he warned when Waters didn't react right away. Eventually though, he shot his younger colleague a glare and left the room.

Ellie took a deep breath. "This turned from mildly annoying to a nightmare quickly." She could tell that Derek was curious, but he didn't ask. "Carroll wants to see you too," he said instead.

"Yeah, I figured. I better go. Thanks."

"No problem. I don't know what he told you, but you're doing okay."

"Thanks again."

A moment later she realized that Waters was still in with the lieutenant. She could hear both men raise their voices, though she couldn't make out words. She never got her coffee either, though that was the least of her concerns right now.

Eventually, Waters yanked the door open and stormed past her, all but pushing her aside. A couple of detectives at their desks pretended not to notice. Ellie knocked on the doorframe.

"Sir? You wanted to see me?"

"Yes. Come in and close the door."

"I'm sure you know why you're here."

"Yes, sir." Ellie wasn't nervous, but she was aware of feeling tired...and sad. They fought hard to convey a zero tolerance for this kind of behavior on the streets and in homes. To have it exhibited by one of their own was terrible, and it was even more depressing to think he might not be the only one. "You want me to tell you what I saw in the break room." He nodded, and so she related what she'd witnessed. She didn't falter and made sure to keep the emotion out of her voice, treat this like she would approach any testimony. Ellie didn't need to worry.

"Thank you. You're aware that there will have to be consequences, so you'll likely have to repeat this to IA."

Ellie wanted to ask many questions, if Officer Potts was going to court, if this had been the first instance. Instead, she said, "Of course."

"Good." He frowned. "Well, this is far from good, but it's where we are now. There is something else I need to ask you."

"No," she said. "He never behaved that way with me." She took a deep breath. Since she was already here, she could just as well seize the moment. "Sir, I know this is a bad time, but regarding the case..."

"Don't tell me it's not closed after all."

"The murder, yes, but I was following a lead..." She had to say it out loud, even though Ellie feared it would sound silly to the lieutenant, coming from her, the least experienced detective in the unit. Beginner's luck, Waters had called her early successes. "Ms. Gilberts committed the murder, but there's a bigger context here. She was working for a man named Hank who apparently has a lot of high-profile clients—like Robertson. He also has a reputation for being extremely cruel. I thought if we could get a team together with Vice, we might be able to get to him, too..."

Lieutenant Carroll mulled her proposal over, or perhaps he just thought that she was incredibly naïve. The silence was stretching too long for her comfort, before he said, "Talk to your source some more, see what they have, and I'll see what I can do. It might be worth a shot."

"Thank you." She would have been incredibly proud if it wasn't for this mess Waters had gotten all of them into.

"All right. That's all. You can go back to work."

Things happened fast. Waters was suspended, Potts was taking a leave as well. Internal Affairs would be in the house the next morning. Meanwhile, Jordan hadn't been able to talk to Ellie. All she'd heard from Derek was about some argument in the break room after Ellie had walked in on him. This was not how she had imagined this partnership would end. Like some of their colleagues, she, too, wondered if they had let his bad behavior slide a few times too many.

Meanwhile she still had a job to do. Nina was with her when she got the ballistics report that came with a puzzling detail about the gun used in the Dinkins and Oswald murders. A post-it note referred to a recent incident in another precinct: The gun they were looking for had been confiscated in another case but was now missing from evidence.

"Everything okay?" Nina asked over her shoulder. She was likely aware of what everyone in the department was talking about in hushed tones, but much to her credit, she didn't comment much.

"Yeah. I'm not sure where we go with this, but it is...interesting."

Jordan pointed at the section of the report she'd just read. She was sure Nina would come to the same conclusion she had.

To her surprise, Nina said, "It's a guess. That doesn't mean someone in law enforcement is behind this."

"Unfortunately, it's hard for someone outside of law enforcement to get their hands on this particular one. It was in an evidence locker."

"Not your division though. Be grateful."

"There's enough going on today. But still, this is disconcerting."

"That someone took out those guys? I don't think so. If they did an amateur job and left all those traces, I'd call that disconcerting."

Jordan turned her chair around to look at the agent. "You think someone was set up? That would create a great alibi for the real killer."

Unless someone had been desperate enough to go down that route. Someone who cared about Isabel Combs—or the other women and girls.

"I can check this out. Why don't you take a break?" Nina suggested. "I'm sure you'd like a few moments with your wife."

Jordan wasn't sure what to make of her sudden shift in mood, but she'd hold that thought, because Nina was right. She really wanted to talk to Ellie, see how she was dealing on this crazy day.

❦

She found Ellie with Maria and Officer Casey Lyons in the parking lot. Apparently neither of them had felt like going into the break room.

Lyons was devastated. "I wish she had talked to me earlier. Look, we always knew he was a jerk. How could we not see this coming?"

"It's not your fault," Ellie assured her after a long look to Jordan. Secretly, they all harbored the same regrets. "Yes, he made jokes that weren't funny, but we didn't know he didn't stop at that. Lieutenant Carroll is on this. He's not going to let it go."

"Yeah." Casey shook her head. "I still don't get it."

"How is she doing?" Jordan asked.

"Terrified of what's going to happen...unsure if she even still wants to be a cop...all of which I can understand," Casey explained. "Some of the boys' club will rally around him."

"Come on," Jordan protested, uncomfortable. "Not here. He never had many friends."

"I'm not talking about you guys, but I've heard some of the rumblings already. Remember what happened when your partner started dating McCarthy? They're not the majority, but you know, squeaky wheel and all."

"She's good," Maria said. "I hope she won't leave because of that one asshole."

"I hope you're not talking about me." Derek had joined them. "Hey, Jordan. There's someone waiting for you."

"Oh crap," she mumbled. "All right, I'm coming."

⁂

Jordan recognized Chelsey Dorman, who was waiting for her with Nina Torres, right away: She was the young woman she had seen pulling the sweater around herself closer, earlier in the coffee shop near Dinkins and Oswald's apartment.

She still looked cold.

"I overheard you talking to Linda," she said. "I couldn't say anything there, but I can tell you something about those men. I'm so glad they are dead."

Jordan caught Nina's thoughtful glance.

"Okay, let's sit down and talk."

They took her to a quieter interview room. Chelsey had to be around twenty, but her posture and expression made her look older. Jordan was reminded of Darla. Darla was safe now, but there were too many like her.

"You knew the men who were killed this week, across from the coffee shop?"

She had to talk to Mulveney, possibly Kim Geller again. It seemed unlikely that they just went about their day without knowing anything that happened right in front of their eyes. Nina had agreed there might be a connection to the upcoming sports event. *Rigley's*, Mulveney's bar, had long been notorious for illegal gambling and betting. There had to be a link, and she was tired of being lied to.

"One of them, Dinkins, I guess. My friend Gina and I met him at a party...I thought he was too old to be hanging around with the frat boys, but that happens sometimes. She liked him. I know that she went out with him a few times, and then...she disappeared. I read all these articles, and..." She swallowed hard, her eyes welling up. "I think something terrible happened to her."

"Did someone report her missing?"

"I don't know her family. They might have. I went to the coffee shop a few times, and that's when I saw him with another girl. That was a couple of days before the murders."

"All right, Chelsey, is there anything else you noticed, anyone he talked to?"

"No. I had a bad feeling, but it didn't really come together until I realized someone had killed them. I wasn't sure what to do...but when I heard you talking to Linda, I thought you might be able to help find Gina."

"We'll do everything we can," Nina assured her. "We'd like you to look at some pictures as well."

Linda came in after her shift as promised, and by the time she left, they had three other pictures on the wall next to Isabel Combs'. Gina Lopez, Ashley Simon, Carly Heller. The women's age ranged from seventeen to twenty. All of them gone missing within the past six months. That was just within two counties.

Jordan had the feeling that the worst was yet to come, and it had already been a pretty awful day.

When they finally agreed to continue the next day, she texted Ellie to meet her at the *D&T*. Ellie texted back that she needed to run an errand first and would see her there.

Chapter Seven

E llie already felt bad when she stepped into Darla's cozy apartment where her son, Jordan Avery Pierson, was enjoying his dinner. Decorating his surroundings with it, seemed a more appropriate description, but both mother and son were having a good time.

"I already know this isn't a social visit, or you'd have picked another time," Darla joked. "If something comes flying, just try to get out of the way in time. That's what I do."

"I'm sorry to bother you again. About this guy, Hank..."

"Yeah." Darla sighed. "I sort of imagined you'd be back. That's got to be frustrating. You just put Lemont away."

"We did. Sometimes..." Ellie didn't finish the sentence. Right now, they had to clean their own house as well. "Anyway, you might have heard about the woman we had to arrest in the Robertson murder. She pulled the trigger, every piece of evidence points to that. She confessed, then said she couldn't remember...I think she's severely traumatized, and that's not just my opinion. It's pretty much out of my hands now, but there is another angle. If we could stop this guy, it'd be a win-win situation. And I'm not yet convinced that she wasn't coerced into killing Robertson. Maybe he pissed off Hank."

"That would be easy to do," Darla agreed somberly. "But it won't be easy to get to him. Put out the word maybe that someone is looking for some high-end entertainment, big shot corporate folks, or celebrities with precarious tastes. An after-game party could work too. If it's high profile enough, he might be interested. I could make a few calls, see if anyone is willing to talk to you."

"I don't want you to do anything dangerous."

"Don't worry. The times when I did almost anything for a donut are over. You and Jordan have helped me a lot. I won't let you down...but you know I have an even better reason."

"Yes, I know. Call me if you find out anything more...and take care."

Ellie stepped out of the way just in time as a spoonful of baby food was catapulted her way, followed by giggles.

She had one more stop on her way before meeting Jordan.

Sam opened the door to her right away. She left it open and went back into the living room of her apartment, as if she didn't care much if Ellie came in or not.

"Hey. I wanted to see how you were doing...with everything."

Sam gave her a shrug. "I guess I have to figure some things out now."

Ellie noticed the buzzing phone on the table. Sam picked it up and turned it off.

"Right now, it's about sixty-forty," she said. "Some of it is good. A few want my head on a silver platter. Would you like some wine? It's not that we have anything to celebrate, but...I felt like it."

"I can imagine." Those weren't just words. Sam hadn't been around long enough to know, but there had been a time when Ellie had depended on a tiny piece of metal as her only weapon. She preferred not to revisit that moment too often—but she could imagine. "But no, thanks. Look...I know we don't know each other that well, but I hope you'll stay. It's your life, and your career, and from what I hear, you're good at this. Don't let one asshole ruin all of it for you."

"Wow." She sat on the edge of the sofa, picking up her glass. "I never thanked you for backing me up today, so...Thank you. I don't even know that I would have talked to the lieutenant if you hadn't come in."

"It's good that you did."

"Not everyone thinks so."

"Then they're wrong." Even though she hadn't meant to stay long, Ellie took a seat as well. "I'm sorry. Of course, it's your decision, whatever you want to do. I wanted to let you know that we're here for you."

"Thanks." Sam gave her a wistful smile. "Are you sure you don't want a glass? You have to make your mind up quick. There might not be any in a bit."

"Do you want to come with me? I'm meeting Jordan, and perhaps some friends, at the *D&T*."

"Thanks, but no. I don't want to go out tonight. But I'm keeping you. It was nice of you to come by."

"They will wait for me. And if one of those calls is from Casey, please, pick up. She's on your side."

Casey had told her earlier that Sam had grown up with her grandmother who had recently passed away. They were silent for a moment, before Sam said, "I don't get it. Why me? Why did he think that he could get away with it, that I might be too weak—?"

"No. You know that for people like that, it's all about them. Whatever he might have thought, it doesn't matter, right? He was wrong. You have a family here. We have your back."

"I appreciate that, but I swear you don't have to stay. If the offer still stands, I might take you up on it another time though."

"Any time. If you want to talk, please call me. Come to think of it, we're having a dinner party soon, and we'd love to have

59

you. If you want, that is. You don't have to tell me anything now, we haven't even set a date yet."

"That's very kind. I'll think about it." Sam accompanied her to the door. "I'll see you."

"Yeah."

There was a moment of hesitation. Ellie waited for Sam to move first, because she hadn't been sure if the gesture was welcome, but then carefully hugged her back.

Some of the tension finally fell away when she walked inside the *D&T*, spotting Jordan at a table near the bar. Jordan got up to greet her with a kiss, and in this place, no one batted an eye if it lasted a little longer.

"Hey. You made it. Are you hungry?"

"God, yes. I thought this day would never end."

"I know what you mean."

Ellie sat and picked up one of the menus. "What are you having? They should do an all-you-can-eat buffet. I feel like I can't make any decisions anymore."

"Let's start with a Thai salad. That's easy."

"What would I do without you?"

Jordan smiled at that, but she didn't give an answer since the waitress stopped at their table to take their orders. Beers arrived quickly. After Ellie had taken a sip, and leaned back into her chair with a sigh, Jordan asked the question.

"How are you?" There was a world of others behind that one.

"Still a bit shocked, I guess. Like everyone. I knew I'd be glad when Waters was gone, but I didn't expect it to happen that way." Even exhausted as she was, she could easily tell what was bothering Jordan. "And no, he never tried anything with me. I've been thinking about this, and remember what Casey said, about Sam losing her grandma? Asshole, he thought she had no one to go to."

"Yeah. Fortunately, it didn't work out that way."

"No. It's just...It makes me so angry. I'm not even the one who—" Ellie stopped when a waitress walked by, but it wasn't the one who had served them. "Now, where is that salad?"

"That's the million-dollar question. And, of course, salad? What happened to you?" Ellie turned around to find herself face to face with her best friend, Kate McCarthy. Behind her was Derek Henderson.

"What are you doing here?" Jordan asked, somewhere between amused and puzzled that their friends had found them. It wasn't that much of a stretch—they had come here together before, and the *D&T*, though the audience was mainly LGBT, was open to everyone.

"A good evening to you, too, Carpenter. Kate said it's been too long since we hung out. Now I realize why that is," Derek quipped.

"Seriously," Kate said, "Derek told me about today. I don't even know what to say to that. It's awful. I mean we deal with some stuff...on the job, and even the occasional jerk, but this is completely different. I hope he's out?"

"Looks that way," Ellie said. "Almost makes me feel guilty, because I'm glad that day came sooner than later."

No one disagreed with her.

⌘

She had been tired earlier but spending time with Jordan and their friends had been reassuring, and food and drinks had helped too. When they were back at home, neither of them felt like sleeping right away. Tomorrow might be another difficult day, but there was still time. Ellie sighed in bliss as Jordan's hands, warm and confident, stole underneath her nightgown, teasing and promising. It came off not much later.

"Not to change the subject. I love the subject," she said, and Jordan chuckled, brushing her lips against Ellie's neck. Momentarily, she was distracted from what she wanted to say. "I might have told a few people we were having a dinner party. Natalie, and Sam...but I think we should invite Ariel too, Jack and Pauline, of course..."

She paused when Jordan's fingers wandered up her thigh.

"Fine with me," Jordan whispered, not distracted at all. Ellie decided it could wait. Everything else could wait. She knew there were things other than the party she'd neglected to mention. Come to think of it, some of them, she should have mentioned to the lieutenant as well—the insinuation that one of his friends might withhold back-up. Not that Waters had many friends at the department.

Enough of that, Ellie told herself. She needed to stop obsessing about him. She and Jordan had kept worse demons at bay.

"Is everything okay?" Jordan, who sensed she was distracted, asked.

"Yes. I love you."

"I love you too." Jordan resumed her task, started kissing her way down Ellie's eager body, capturing all of her attention. One more thing Ellie had found out she loved: Married sex.

Much later, even though her body was as relaxed as it could be, her mind couldn't follow enough to let her sleep. She turned, trying to be silent not to wake Jordan, but as it was, she didn't have to.

"Can't sleep?" Jordan asked, quietly stating the obvious.

"I still don't understand how we couldn't see it. I hate this, you know? I mean, we've seen some horrible things." She knew she didn't need to specify. "And it was hard, but we got through it. I know I got through it because I had my chosen family—my friends, and you. We always had that to come back to, right?"

"Yeah. I know."

This had been a certainty after every traumatic experience, every close call they'd faced. They might be dealing with it differently, but this was something they'd always had in common.

"Coming back to work. I know it saved both of us. I remember exactly what it felt like to put on the uniform again. I don't know that it's the same for Sam."

"Well, that's also up to us, isn't it? Atwood and his gang are not in the majority, and they know it."

"I hope you're right."

"Carroll won't tolerate this shit, and I know Sergeant Bristol is the same. If those guys want trouble, they're going to get it."

Ellie snuggled back in her arms, comforted—for now.

Jordan had done her best to assure Ellie everything would be okay. She thought she'd done a decent job, even though there was no denying this was a complex situation that would have implications for everyone. Still, she managed to get to work before Nina arrived and do a quick check on Natalie Morgan. There wasn't much to be found, but it looked like she said who she was. She had gotten a few parking tickets but appeared to be a law-abiding citizen otherwise. That was at least something good to tell Ellie.

She looked at her phone, oddly aware of the lack of texts from Kathryn. In the beginning, her biological mother's behavior had bordered on stalking, making Jordan wonder if she should take action. After several difficult conversations, they had come to a cease-fire. Neither she nor Jim was invited to the wedding, and things had gotten calm. Maybe too calm, but at the moment, Jordan had enough on her plate to add another thing to worry about.

Nina still wasn't around yet, so she started organizing notes and folders on the missing women.

"Still no sign of Combs." Everyone in their unit was used to the lieutenant sneaking up on them every once in a while, so she didn't even startle.

"No," she said, suppressing a sigh.

"Come into my office for a moment?"

Jordan got up to follow him. Inside Carroll's office, they both remained standing. There wasn't enough news to require sitting.

"Any hint as to who killed those two men?" he asked.

"Not yet. With Combs out there, the focus has slightly shifted." Or it kept shifting whenever Nina introduced a new aspect of her investigation. "We know there are more women, and it's likely that there's a connection to upcoming sports events."

"The pre-season game." Carroll winced.

"Yeah." Jordan didn't blame him. She didn't care much about the games, but they swept a lot of people into town. Enough to put the locals on alert—law enforcement, and criminals who didn't want to share with out-of-town players.

"When you asked me about Harding getting a new partner, was that in any way related to what Officer Potts reported?" he asked.

Jordan spun around, surprised, though she realized she shouldn't have been.

"No. I swear. Not everyone's a good teacher, and I thought she could benefit more from working with Detective Doss." It was a good thing that Ellie never learned about her meddling—Jordan was, a little too late, aware it had been uncalled for, and only unnecessarily complicated things.

"I see."

She followed his gaze, and through the open blinds, they could see the men and woman who had just walked in. "Excuse me please, I'll have to have a word with the folks from IA."

"Of course."

Nina Torres arrived the moment she sat back down.

"Sorry, I'm late, but I had to clear something with your A. D.A. How about we go bust some bad guys?"

"Sounds like a plan."

Ellie wasn't sure how the day would play out, and who would want to talk to her when. She started by organizing what she had found out from Darla, and her conversations with Gilbert's attorney. They had found out earlier that an assault case against Owens, seven years ago, had been dismissed, and apparently, he'd followed the law ever since. It bothered her that she couldn't do anything for Gilbert at this point, but if they were to save other women from the same fate, there was some hope at least.

Sam hadn't called her, but perhaps she'd join them tonight. Once she had something in order she would be able to present to the lieutenant, she went over other files on her desk. Ellie didn't think Carroll would have much time today, with IA in the house.

She also took a short break to call Madeline. Everyone else, she could call or text later, but her mother's friend was the only one who might appreciate a warning before meeting Natalie.

"Ellie, it's so nice to hear from you. How's married life?"

"It's been great, thank you." In fact, it was the easiest, most beautiful part of her life. She was truly happy, all the other challenges notwithstanding. "The reason I'm calling is that we'll have a dinner with a few people, because...I'd like to introduce you all to someone." This had happened so suddenly, it felt strange to relate it to someone other than Jordan who had met Natalie already.

"That sounds mysterious."

"It really isn't. I found out a few days ago that I have a...half sister."

Madeline had been friends with her parents for a long time. Maybe Ellie was even hoping there could be a slight chance...

"How?" Madeline asked, puzzled. "I mean...I don't claim to know everything about Pat and Meri, but I know they married young, and there is no way—am I getting this completely wrong? I'm sorry."

"Natalie told me her mother was in a relationship with Dad before he met Mom. It's all...plausible, and Madeline, she showed me a picture. This is real."

"Wow. This is a surprise."

"Yes, but a good one. I have a sister! I found someone who's actually related to me. She seems very nice, of course I have only met her a couple of times, but I'd really like her to meet my other family."

"I'm glad to be a part of that. You must have checked her story, too?"

"Jordan did," Ellie said, hoping this would convince her mother's friend. "I know, this is crazy, but she's for real. And her mother died not long ago, so I can...relate to that."

"Of course. I'm happy for you, and I'd love to meet her. Just tell me when."

"We're still planning, but I'll let you know. Thank you. I have to go now," she said when she saw Lieutenant Carroll open the door of his office, coming out with the woman from Internal Affairs.

"How's Mulveney behaving?" Nina Torres asked when they were in the car, on the way to meet a possible witness. It wasn't the question Jordan had expected, though she wasn't surprised Nina had put two and two together.

"So far, so good. He's been a little sketchy on the details, but at least he gave us the sports connection."

"Yeah, that was a good one."

"So where are we going?" Jordan felt like Torres hadn't been generous with that information.

"I called in a few favors, and one of the numbers Dinkins called belongs to a name that rings a bell," Nina explained. "I believe this guy has some answers as to the whereabouts of Combs' and the others." She reached behind her seat to produce a folder. "Low level, so no one's going to come bailing him out anytime soon. There's a good chance he'll be interested in a conversation."

Jordan leafed through the file, skimming over the man's rap sheet.

"Precious. If he's so low level, why do you think he can help us?"

"I know the type," Nina said confidently. "With those events coming up, they'll need a lot of foot soldiers." Jordan had come to disturbing conclusions on her own, before Nina added, "After they already lured them in."

Busting that guy sounded better and better.

The house was fairly run-down, in a neighborhood where most other houses looked the same. A few rackety stairs led up to the front door. There was a black truck parked in front of it. Jordan and Nina exited the car and went to the front door. Nina knocked. There was no answer, though they heard noises from inside. One especially made them step away from the door and tuck themselves against the wall on either side.

Just before he started shooting.

From the sounds of it, he wasn't all that interested in a conversation.

"Don't be stupid," Nina yelled between shots. "We just want to talk to you!"

"I don't want to talk to you!" He stopped shooting though. Jordan wasn't getting her hopes up high yet.

"You should. We can help you. I know you got into some bad shit, but it's not you we are after."

There was a shadow behind the door, and Jordan gripped her own gun tighter.

"What do you want?"

"Talk about your friend Dinkins. Or perhaps you knew him as Ted Hart."

"Haven't seen him in years."

"Cut the crap. We know you called him a few weeks ago. Look, if you help us find those women, we might even forget that you were shooting at us a second ago. Otherwise...let's just say if Dinkins' friends find you first, and they think you talked to the police, it will be a lot worse."

He came out onto the porch, holding his hands up. Nina straightened, pointing his gun at him as she walked up the stairs, Jordan behind her.

All of a sudden, he dropped his hands, reaching for...whatever it was; Nina was faster, pulling the trigger.

Chapter Eight

J ordan replayed the moment in her mind a few times, coming to the same conclusion. Nina had no choice, did she? He had greeted them with gunfire, before even knowing why they were here, so she had reason to assume he would not cooperate. She had called for backup and an ambulance. The man was dead.

"Sorry," Nina mumbled as she holstered her gun. "I didn't expect it to become this messy."

"You had no choice. He was shooting at us."

However, Torres wasn't looking for reassurance from her.

"I'm aware, but thanks. Let's make sure the scene is secured, and then we'll take a look at the house."

"You really think he knew where the women are?"

"I think he wasn't as prepared for eventualities as Dinkins and Oswald. We might still get lucky."

The officers arriving were Wes Martin and Libby Marshall, and two younger men Jordan had seen before at the *Night Shift*, Yang and Ennis. From Potts' class, she realized. Wes and Libby joined her and Nina as they searched the modest two-story house from top to bottom. Upstairs, there was a bedroom with a TV and DVR, a few USB drives on the nightstand. Jordan wondered what might be on them, wincing at the possibilities.

A bathroom next door showed no hint of another person—a shaving kit, some over the counter painkillers. They bagged the drives and continued. This time, the closet didn't contain any surprises, just pants and shirts hung haphazardly on mismatched hangers.

Downstairs, the kitchen was stocked with mostly cans and frozen goods. A few six packs of a cheap beer brand, and some vodka. There were stairs leading to a small cellar with the heating system, a washer and dryer. A door was secured with a lock, the key still in it.

"Go ahead," Nina muttered. "If somebody shoots at you, you know I'm faster."

In spite of what was probably meant to reassure, Jordan felt tense when she turned the key and carefully opened the door. She flinched at the sight revealed. The person on the other side of that door wasn't going to do them any harm.

It was Chelsey's friend Gina.

She was alive.

<hr />

"I thought you'd be busier today," Officer Chris Atwood remarked as he walked by Ellie's desk, after dropping off a file for Detective Doss. Maria looked up from her computer screen, watching the scene with interest.

"I'm working. Aren't you?"

"Say, what's it like to destroy someone's reputation? It would have been so easy, Harding. You could have told the truth."

Here we go.

"What the hell are you talking about?" She had told Jordan and Kate before that there was no point in answering to gossip, but she was about to reach her breaking point. Chris Atwood thought gay marriage was immoral and a sign of end times. It didn't surprise her in the least that he'd take Waters' side. "If this is about your friend, I told the truth to everyone who asked me."

"Really? The guy was weeks away from retirement."

"Yeah. He should have thought about that. He should have used his brain before doing any of it."

"Oh, come on, we all know about Potts—"

"Shut up," she said. "Since you're so worried about my work, why don't you let me get back to it?"

Maria Doss laughed when he stalked out of the room. "That was impressive. I'm not sure what Jordan was worried about. You don't let anyone mess with you."

"Wait. Did she say anything? When?" Ellie could think of a couple of times that Derek Henderson had appeared out of nowhere during an argument with Waters.

"Don't worry about it. She didn't need to say anything."

"Sorry." Ellie sighed. "Waters has friends. Imagine that."

"Not that many. Atwood's dad and Waters' brother hang out together. I think it ends there."

"Let's hope."

She picked up her phone and answered when she saw the call came from Jordan.

"Before you hear from anyone else, I just wanted to let you know we're okay..."

"If you didn't want me to worry, that's not the way to go about it. What happened?"

"Something good. We found one of the women."

Ellie decided it wasn't the moment to bother Jordan—or anyone today, for that matter, with Atwood's stupid antics.

A couple of minutes on the phone with Ellie was the only break Jordan got. Gina was disoriented and freezing, but she was coherent enough to answer a few questions, before she was taken away in the ambulance. Those few minutes already spoke of unthinkable horrors.

Libby went to the hospital with her while Jordan and Nina finished up the search, then joined them after a doctor had tended to the young woman and performed necessary tests.

Gina confirmed that she had met Dinkins at the frat party. She'd been flattered he took an interest in her.

"At first, I went along with everything." She blinked as if that had been so long ago she almost couldn't remember. Torres' features were set in a tense expression. "Then he told me that he owed some powerful people money, and they had threatened him. There...was a way I could help him." Tears ran down her face. "How could I be so stupid? He said he loved me, and if I loved him too, I'd do this, make sure they wouldn't kill him."

"He let other men rape you," Nina said.

The woman nodded. Jordan thought that clarity of language was of utmost importance. Place the blame where it belonged. She hated this case with a passion. Whoever had killed Dinkins and Oswald, she couldn't help thinking they had done society a favor. Those were still murders she had to investigate, though, and chances were the killer—or killers—didn't care all that much about the women.

"There's nothing stupid about it," she said firmly. "You met a guy at a party, started dating him—you couldn't expect this to happen." Except he had targeted her. How many others?

Gina continued. "He was always so jealous. He bought me a phone, wanted me to destroy mine. Whenever I asked questions, he said it was just the two of us now, and when I wanted to leave, he told me that the same people that threatened him would come after my family and friends! I didn't know what to do!"

"How long did this go on?" Torres asked quietly.

"Until about five days ago. I think. I lost count in the dark. This guy came over, and they were talking, about someone called Ray. Then he said I had to go with him. I didn't want to and he...hit me. I hadn't been feeling well before, and I passed out. I woke up in that cellar."

"Dinkins' place, where was it?" Jordan had a bad feeling, and it was instantly confirmed when Gina described the area where Dinkins had taken her. It wasn't the place where they had held Isabel Combs. There was another house or apartment somewhere, for the same gruesome purpose.

"Thank you, Gina, you've helped us a lot."

Out in the hallway, Jordan noticed that Torres looked pale in the light of the halogen lamps. She didn't blame her.

"Are you okay?"

Nina shook her head. "Hell, no. We have to look for another place, and we still have no idea where Isabel is—or this Ray person. You know what, I could really use a drink."

"No kidding. You want to go after we wrap things up here...and regroup?"

"I'd love to. This is the most welcoming department I've ever worked with."

"Really? I'm sorry for the other experiences then." She wondered if Bethany had ever mentioned their previous relationship. "Let me just find out what Ellie is up to."

Before she could do that, her cell phone vibrated in her hand, announcing the arrival of a lengthy text message from Kathryn. Jordan decided that she wasn't going to deal with it today and made her call.

Ellie sounded tired. "I didn't think you'd want to go out tonight. I'm kind of tired, and you must be too. Besides, you have yet to reassure me that you're okay like you promised."

Okay might be relative after everything she'd heard today, but Jordan reminded herself that Ellie was having a number of tough days as well.

"Just one drink," she said. "You didn't have dinner, did you?"

"No. I guess I can do one drink. I'll see you later. *Night Shift*?"

"Sounds good. Thank you. How did it go with IA?"

"Okay, I guess. They asked a few questions about the incident and Waters' general conduct, and I told them what I could."

"All right. I love you." She changed gears quickly when the phone started vibrating again seconds after she'd ended the call. "For Christ's sake, why?"

"I'm not sure if I should ask," Nina commented.

"Neither am I, but dinner is a go. Ellie will join us once she's done. I guess we'll get back to it tomorrow. The lab's bound to have something for us from the house."

"Yeah. Let's go."

"How long have you been on this case?" Jordan asked after they'd sat down at the bar. She was quite certain that Torres' involvement was no coincidence. She didn't just randomly make the connection after the murders—she had likely been on Dinkins' and Oswald's trail for a while. Otherwise, she wouldn't have been able to pull one of their cohorts out of the proverbial hat so quickly. That, and Jordan could see she was tired. Exhaustion from a case that wouldn't end she could understand. She'd had one of those, and it had come with high costs.

"Too long. Too many women missing, turning up dead, or not at all...today was a good day, believe me. I'm not going to shed any tears over the guy I shot."

"I get that." Ellie was nowhere to be seen yet, and she hadn't texted or called again. Jordan was sipping her beer slowly, while Nina downed a shot.

"Frankly, a shot to the head is a pretty easy way out for the other guys too." She signaled the bartender for another shot. "I know it's your job to know who did it, but unless they are in the same business, I don't care."

Jordan wondered if asking her to slow down a bit would sound patronizing. She could understand the impulse to drink the images and implications away for a few hours. From experience, she knew they'd still be there the next morning, but then again, that was probably nothing new for Nina.

"They were too damn clever, getting away each time," she said. "Not this time, though."

There was something in her tone that startled Jordan. She wasn't sure if there was an actual hint in that, or if the narrative had simply triggered something in her own memory. There were monsters out there. It could feel cathartic to wish them dead. They didn't go there unless they absolutely had to, right?

"But that's enough about me. You and your partner have an amazing track record. You recently got married. What else? Is now a good moment to ask about the text message?"

Now, Jordan wanted a shot too. She shrugged. "Not really work related. My biological mother. It's a long story."

"They're all long stories, aren't they? Since you're making that distinction, I assume you haven't always been on speaking terms."

Still no Ellie. Where was she? Jordan took another sip of her beer. Right now, she wished she had gone with Ellie's suggestion to go home. She understood Nina was trying to get away from the horrors of the day. She was questioning her methods.

"It's been better than it was. I should really check on Ellie."

"Yeah, you do that."

Jordan couldn't help thinking that she was getting a lot of clues tonight—she wasn't yet sure about the picture.

I'm just leaving, Ellie texted as she walked towards her car. *I'll be there in ten.*

For a brief moment, she thought about calling Sam, but decided against it. The case Jordan and Agent Torres were working on might not be something she felt like talking about tonight—and Ellie assumed that after today's incident, the evening wouldn't completely pass without shop talk.

She didn't have the chance to present her notes to the lieutenant yet, so perhaps she could run them past Jordan, and if she was interested, Torres as well. Maybe everything Brandi Gilbert had endured wouldn't be for nothing after all.

"Hey, Harding. You're going home already? Don't have work to do?"

"Give it a rest," she muttered, unlocking the car door. She jumped when Atwood slammed it shut, crowding her against the side of the car.

"You think you're so clever, right? You remember what Cliff said. He might be out, but a few of us are still here. And we don't like drama queens and liars."

"I don't like *you*," she snapped. "Now get lost or I'll kick you in the balls. I'm not joking."

Apparently, Atwood believed that she could because he backed up a step.

"Don't you ever forget that you need us when you're out there by yourself," he warned. "Bitch."

"Yeah, right. Amazing vocabulary you have there."

When he was gone, Ellie opened the door, sat inside, and started the car, then killed the engine when she realized her hands were shaking. She wouldn't give him the satisfaction of having an accident on top of it all. This was only confirmation—they had indulged the likes of him and Waters too long. No more. Tomorrow she'd talk to Carroll, and he would certainly have a word with Sergeant Bristol.

When she felt a bit less jittery, Ellie pulled out of the parking lot. Maria was right—she wouldn't let anyone mess with her, especially when they threatened someone she loved.

Nina had excused herself and gone to the bathroom when Ellie finally arrived.

"Hey. What took you so long? I'm sorry. I didn't mean it like that. What's wrong? I'm okay, I swear."

"We still have so much to do with that stupid dinner party," Ellie said, her eyes welling up.

"If it's too much, we don't have to—what happened?"

Taking a deep breath, Ellie eyed the assortment of shot glasses on the counter. "I'll tell you, but you go first. What did I miss?"

"I just had one beer. So?"

Ellie sat on a barstool. "I'm sorry for being so dramatic. Atwood isn't happy I told the truth about Waters, and with everything else, it slipped my mind, but back in the break room, Waters told me to be careful, if we needed backup at some point in the future. I thought he was just talking. Now I'm not so sure anymore."

"I'm so sorry. We'll take it to the lieutenant tomorrow, first thing in the morning."

Jordan felt silly for telling her the other day that everything would be fine. In her defense, she'd been missing an important part of the puzzle, but she couldn't blame Ellie either. Too much had happened in the past few days, and yes, there was still the dinner party—and it mattered, sharing this important development in Ellie's life with their friends and family.

"Yeah. I guess we have no choice."

After another fairly sleepless night, the next couple of days passed without any further incident. Both Lieutenant Carroll and Sergeant Bristol confirmed that they wouldn't take threats from one cop to another lightly.

Ellie got her chance to talk to Carroll about her findings as well. He agreed that there needed to be more personnel on this, and he called Derek, Jordan, and Agent Torres into the meeting as well.

The more people this involved, the more nervous she got, especially at this moment. She was still fairly new to this particular unit. Of course, Waters was the only one to blame for his premature exit, but he had been her partner, and there would likely be new scrutiny, especially after she'd brought new complaints. In all of it, she still hadn't managed to talk to Jordan about having involved Darla.

However, when Carroll gave the word to her, Ellie knew exactly what she wanted to say.

"My source tells me that this Hank has been around for a while, elusive, running things mostly from out of town. But he pays attention when a lot of wealthy people come to town. He goes beyond the traditional escort services, focusing on high profile clients with violent tastes. There are still unanswered questions about the Brandi Gilbert case."

"The pre-season game could be big business for this guy, then," Jordan surmised, and Torres nodded.

"Since we have found no connection at all between him, and Dinkins and Oswald, it might not be too much of a stretch to think they stepped on his toes," she added. "If their boss thinks he could benefit from a turf war, there might be more bodies."

"That's what we're all trying to avoid," Carroll said.

"I could go and talk to Gilbert once more," Ellie offered. "We could also put out the word that someone's looking for entertainment for an after-game party."

"If that's going to be me, I could also get in touch with a CI of mine." Derek leaned back in his seat. "He might have heard some chatter."

Part of her was still astonished at the way this was going. Most of all, Ellie was relieved that she could come back to work and find that she was still part of the family, that whatever Waters and Atwood came up with were nothing but lies. That same family would come through for Samantha Potts.

Chapter Nine

I n the light of day, Jordan wondered if she had misunderstood Nina's words. She had shared her impressions with Ellie who reminded her to trust her instincts—and then it was finally the weekend, and they could plan the party over breakfast in bed. The list kept growing.

"This almost looks like a carbon copy of the wedding. Do we need a cake, too?" Jordan joked.

"Hm." Ellie gave the list a thoughtful look. "A cake would be good. I don't know." She shook her head. "We've been so busy, whenever I have a moment to think about this, it still feels completely unreal. I mean, I like her, but she's still a stranger. I don't even know what it's supposed to feel like. I know I don't want to scare her away."

"You won't, I promise. You're the kindest person I know. Why would that scare her away?"

"You make it sound so easy." Ellie sounded wistful.

"She seems...uncomplicated. You two will be fine. Are we okay with the list now?"

"Why, you have any plans?"

"Yes," Jordan said, taking the coffee cup out of her hands, leaning in to kiss her. Ellie willingly surrendered the list for the moment.

"I like where this is going," she said.

Natalie called on Sunday evening. Ellie had been sitting on the couch, some music playing in the background while Jordan was in the shower. The weekend had done wonders to help clear her thoughts, regarding the job, and other things. They had talked about the connection between their cases, but then simply taken time for themselves.

Together. She still marveled at the fact that they had been able to leave all those reservations and bad decisions in earlier relationships behind and move forward to this point. Live together, get married. Sometimes, she couldn't help thinking what it would have been like, had Ariel come to live with them. Ellie felt a bit melancholic, but not as deeply sad as she had in the beginning. Ariel was happy and had the support of a loving family. That was all they'd ever wanted for her, and they were still able to keep in touch.

Her phone rang from somewhere in the depth of her purse, and she got up to get it.

"Hey, Natalie, how are you?"

"I'm good, thank you. Um...do you have a minute?"

"Yes, of course. I'm glad you called. About that party, would next Saturday be okay with you?"

"Sure, that will be fine. Ellie..." She sounded serious. "There's something I need to tell you."

"Is everything all right with you?" *Please, no bad news. I just found her.*

"Yes, I'm good. Look, I really had a hard time trying to decide whether I should tell you. You were right, we don't know each other all that much, but...I think you deserve to know. I went out for a drink yesterday." She paused.

Ellie wasn't sure whether she should be concerned or irritated.

"Natalie, what's wrong?"

"I saw Jordan. With another woman. I'm so, so sorry, but I had to tell you."

"When was that?" Ellie asked, then shook her head at herself. That was not what she'd meant to ask.

"A few days ago, at a bar...They looked pretty close."

"This is a misunderstanding. If you had waited a little longer, you would have seen that I was there too. The woman you saw is an FBI agent."

"Are you sure?"

Irritation was starting to gain over concern. "Natalie, please, you have to trust me a little. Listen. Jordan would never do that. They were working on a case, having a drink afterwards. It happens sometimes."

"Yeah, I'm sure it does. I'm so relieved! I'm sorry I worried you for nothing. Am I still invited?"

"Yes, of course. You're the guest of honor. And there's nothing to worry about, but thanks for looking out for me."

"Always. You're the only little sister I have."

"Like I said, thank you, and believe me: This is not an issue."

"I get it," Natalie said ruefully. "I really messed up this big sister thing, didn't I? I promise I'll do better. I know that you're in love, and just got married, but sometimes—"

"Please, forget about it. It's fine."

"Thank you. I can't wait to meet all your friends."

"We'll see you Saturday then. At six."

Ending the call, Ellie wondered if everyone around her had lost their mind. Fortunately, Jordan returned from the bathroom that moment, and Ellie had to get up and pull her close for a deep kiss.

"You missed me?"

"Oh yes."

"Who called?"

"Natalie. I told her about the party."

"And?"

"Nothing. She's still fine with it, so I guess it's a go." It wasn't a perfect decision, but Ellie didn't want to have a conversation that might bring up painful mistakes for Jordan. She wasn't that insecure. It bothered her that Natalie would jump to conclusions like that, and she hoped she had been firm enough in rejecting them. Maybe their surprise reunion had been a little too smooth, and they both had to realize that they'd have to learn a lot more about each other.

Ellie's resolve lasted until the next morning, when she confessed to Jordan over the first sip of coffee.

"I'm sorry. I know you probably didn't want to hear this, but I can't keep secrets from you. I don't want to."

Jordan seemed a bit puzzled, though fortunately not offended.

"I understand. It's okay, but...why didn't she come over? I would have introduced Torres, and you were on your way."

"That's what I told her. I don't know. Maybe we're both trying a little too hard. We might be related, but we're still strangers."

"I know how that feels." Jordan sighed. "That reminds me, Kathryn sent some texts again. She wants to know if we had a nice honeymoon. Regarding Natalie, that's even more extreme—you two have never met. I understand overcompensating."

"I so understand that. You're not mad at me?"

"Why would I be? You know I'm not going to hook up with Torres, right?"

"Of course I know that."

"Let's forget about it," Jordan suggested. "If she'll be around, and it looks that way, you'll figure out how to communicate."

"Like you did with Kathryn."

"Sort of. But you'll be okay. You're starting off with a clean slate."

"True. I'm glad I told you."

"Me too."

***

"Glad" was a relative term. Jordan was fairly proud of herself for not letting her own emotions get in the way and instead focusing on what this news meant for Ellie. Fortunately, they were in a good place that allowed them to brush off Natalie's misperception.

When she had cheated on Bethany, it was because she'd wanted out and had been unable to achieve that goal in a mature and adult fashion. She and Bethany had never been in that good, secure place where the other person felt one hundred percent safe. And it didn't matter anymore, because whatever Natalie thought she might have seen, she got it wrong.

Her rush to judgment was startling, but most likely she wanted to be a loyal and reliable presence in Ellie's life. But why those charges specifically, and why had she come to the *Night Shift*? Coincidence?

"You answered your mother?" Nina Torres asked as she put a coffee in front of Jordan. Startled out of her musings, she realized that her phone was buzzing again. This time, it was Pauline telling her that she and Jack would be at the party.

"Why is everybody so interested in my private life?"

She hadn't quite meant to say it out loud, but Nina's amused smile told her she had.

"It's nothing personal. We are interested in other people's personal lives because we all want to live vicariously or remind ourselves that it could always be worse. Sorry, that sounded better in my head." She took a sip of her own coffee. "We're all set for your guy to go in?"

They'd had another meeting earlier, including a couple of Vice detectives. One of them had heard the name Hank mentioned once, but no one had ever seen him.

Derek was preparing to make contact with someone from the list Darla had provided for Ellie, names further down on the ladder. He would pose as an associate of a wealthy businessman who was in town to discuss sponsoring but also wanted a private party for after the game.

"Soon," Jordan answered her. This was all going fast. They didn't have any additional clues regarding the gun that had disappeared from an evidence locker in another precinct. Nina had asked around as promised, not turning up much. The gun had originally been filed in the case of a shootout in a parking lot, handled by a couple of detectives by the names of Shriver and Cortez. According to the paperwork it had never been touched again.

If the theory of a turf war was still valid, had one of their own decided to put their finger on the scale? A few weeks ago, she would have sworn it wasn't possible, but one of her colleagues was suspended, because he had assaulted another officer, and Chris Atwood had faced a reprimand.

"What about the officer who reported the assault? How is she doing?"

Torres had mostly refrained from even mentioning Potts, but she seemed concerned.

"She's okay, considering. She'll come back to work next week."

"That's good. You need some sort of normalcy."

"Yeah. What about you?"

"Me, why? I'm fine. You were there. The bastard locked a woman in his basement, and he shot at us. I haven't been losing any sleep, and neither has my supervisor."

"Good."

One reason why a gun from an evidence locker might show up at the murder scene of a couple of human traffickers—someone had enough.

The problem was, in neither scenario could they just let it go. An execution was different from the situation she'd witnessed, Nina killing the man in justified self-defense.

She pushed the thought aside when she saw Ellie walking in, heading straight for Jordan's desk.

"You're both here, good," she said. "Do you have a moment?"

For a split-second, Jordan was reminded of Natalie's near accusations, and she wondered if Ellie would be bothered by her drinking coffee with Nina Torres. That was ridiculous though. She wanted Ellie to be happy and have the best possible relationship with her sister. That didn't mean they couldn't point out when she was wrong.

"Sure, what do you have?" Nina asked.

"I've been going over Gina's statement, and she mentioned a Ray."

"Yeah, the go-between for Dinkins," Jordan remembered. "Why?"

"The main witness in the Robertson case, who saw Brandi Gilbert standing over his boss's body with the gun? His name is Raymond Owens. Now, that could be a coincidence, but I'm not so sure. I ran a check on him a while ago. The only thing I found was an assault charge that was dropped, seven years ago. What was strange, though, the first thing Brandi Gilbert said to me was 'have you arrested him yet?'"

"We need a little bit more than that," Nina said. "It's interesting, though. Gina never saw Ray, but perhaps you could try with Gilbert again. In the meantime, we see what happens if we drop his name with the folks Darla Pierson gave us. Thanks, Harding."

"You're welcome. So...I'll try to go see her as soon as possible. Brandi Gilbert, I mean."

"Yes, you do that."

Ellie was barely hiding her excitement. Watching her leave, Jordan allowed herself a moment of pride and affection for her. She had always known Ellie would find a place and make a name for herself in this unit. Knowing Ellie wanted her as much as she wanted this career was still a miracle to her.

Chapter Ten

Ellie barely suppressed a flinch when she stepped into the room with Brandi Gilbert. She could already see how the time in jail had hardened her, or perhaps it was something that had been there before, something that had allowed her to survive so far. She wished she could turn back time for her, to a moment where she could reverse course.

"How are you doing?" she asked.

"What do you think?" Gilbert shook her head. "I didn't think you'd come back here. Isn't your case closed?"

"I was hoping we could talk."

"Whatever. I'm not going anywhere."

"I know Mr. McKenzie talked to you about the possibility that you could be transferred to another facility."

"Not going to happen. I'm not insane enough."

"Why do you say that?"

"Look, lady, you're wasting your time, and mine. I have nothing more to say to you, or Mr. McKenzie."

"We are both trying to help you—and the other women. Hank, Robertson, Owens—we know they all did terrible things."

"Do you? Yet here I am, in prison. Which is probably for the best. At least I always know where the next meal is coming from, and if I keep my head down, they leave me alone."

This time, Ellie did flinch. She wasn't ready to give up.

"We found a missing girl. She was kidnapped, locked in a basement. We think Owens might have been aware."

"Aware." Brandi laughed bitterly. "I don't know what you want from me. I'm not getting out, and like I said, it's not the worst thing. I talk too much, one of his girls in here might get wind of it. It's not that hard to smuggle a knife in."

"I need your help, Brandi. We can stop them. All of them, but I can't do it without you."

"I told McKenzie already there is nothing to tell. Don't you talk to each other?"

"Please. There are other girls out there right now. I am so sorry that we couldn't help you before. You're not insane, but you deserve to get help. More than you can in here."

When Brandi looked up at her again, there were tears in her eyes.

"You know, sometimes I wish I was. But it's all clear. It's what these bastards do, lock us up, in the dark, sometimes without food and water, and then there's...the other stuff."

Having read Gina's statement, Ellie knew exactly what she was talking about.

"The girl that you found, is she going to make it?"

That could mean many things. "I believe so," Ellie said, hoping she could provide at least the tiniest bit of comfort with her answer.

Brandi shook her head, tears still running down her face.

"I don't think you can protect me. They said that no one can, but what does it change at this point? Owens is tight with Hank, has been before he got the gig with Robertson. He always booked the girls when Robertson wanted to party...and some of his friends as well."

"Did you ever meet with Hank in person? You know where he is?"

"He has his people to run things, but when it's the important clients, he may get involved."

"Okay. Did you ever hear that he clashed with other..." Ellie wasn't quite sure how to word it.

"Pimps? Oh, sure, all the time. But those were on a smaller scale. He wants it all, run the streets and the parties in those expensive hotel rooms."

Ellie mulled this over for a moment. The pieces were coming together. This didn't sound like a guy who would easily accept someone else encroaching on their territory.

"This is very helpful, thank you, Brandi. Look, you don't have to answer this, but there's something I keep wondering about. Why Mr. Robertson?"

There was a long pause in which Ellie thought she'd lost her again, then Brandi said, "Because Owens made me. It was about money, I don't know all of it. He said prison was the best someone like me could hope for, and that if I ever told anyone, Hank would send me off to someplace worse than anything they'd done before." She laughed bitterly. "There are some things worse than dying."

"You're not going to die," Ellie said firmly. "I'll have to talk to a few people. We'll make sure that you're safe in here. Let me make some calls."

She left the prison and took out her cell phone the moment she sat in her car. McKenzie was quite enthusiastic when Ellie asked him to meet.

"Thanks, Detective. I really appreciate your initiative."

Fairly emboldened, she called the A.D.A. next. Valerie Esposito's reaction was a bit more sobering.

"I could meet you in an hour, but don't expect too much," she warned. "Gilbert has changed her story a few times now. She shot him, she can't remember, now this Owens guy made her do it. That's not going to look good."

"Honestly, at the moment, I don't care what it looks like. Raymond Owens likely knew about Gina, and he might know where Isabel Combs is. He is the link between those cases."

"And for that, you have the slightly vague statement of a woman who was held in a dark cellar, drugged, probably tortured, and she might have overheard talk about a guy named Ray. I'm sorry, Ellie, that's still thin."

"I know, but Brandi Gilbert is afraid. That has never changed, and we need to protect her."

Valerie sighed. "I'll see what I can do. I'll meet you and McKenzie in an hour."

"Oh, while we're at it, I'd like a search warrant for Owens' apartment."

"Would you now? I'd like an all-inclusive vacation at a luxury resort in the Bahamas, and a date with Halle Berry, but it's not very likely at the moment."

Ellie waited.

After a heavy sigh, Esposito added, "I'll look into it."

"Thank you. We're going to ask him to come in, talk, see if he's open to giving up this Hank guy."

"Good luck," Valerie said.

"Thanks. I can use it."

"No kidding."

***

Owens sat in the precinct's waiting area, getting to his feet when he saw Ellie. He didn't look too happy.

"Mr. Owens, thank you for coming in," she greeted him. "There are a few things to clarify. Come with me please."

He followed her but kept arguing all the way to the interrogation room.

"What's to clarify? The bitch is behind bars, where she belongs. What else is there?"

"Like I said. A few things." Ellie opened the door, and he walked past her into the room, slumping into a chair. After closing the door again, she sat across from him and opened the folder on the table, showing him a photograph from the house where Nina and Jordan had found Gina.

"Let's forget about Ms. Gilbert for a moment. Do you know where this is?"

"No. Should I? You asked me here for that? Lady, I have a job to do."

"What kind of job is that? Providing entertainment for your clients? Look, we know you're the one who corresponded with the owner of the escort service, not Mr. Robertson. We also know you did the same for a handful of other clients of yours. That in itself isn't looking so good, but we're more interested in Hank."

There was a minute reaction in his expression before he went back to the same condescending smile.

"I have friends who know girls who like to party. What are you going to do about it?"

"I'm only interested in those who are underage...and those who are forced to be there. Like Brandi Gilbert, Isabel Combs, Gina Lopez...We hear you had some problems with Mr. Robertson over money...he ends up dead. We now have a version that's quite different from the one you gave us. Brandi tells us you forced her to kill him. Another guy mentions your name in connection with the escort business, and he winds up dead, too, along with his partner. If you don't start talking soon, you might end up the fall guy in all of this. Frankly, Mr. Owens, I don't care. It's up to you."

"You have the words of a bunch of whores," he spat. "That's not going to do anything."

Ellie slowly got to her feet. First, she needed to make a bit of distance from this toxic individual. Second, her blazer falling open slightly revealed her badge and gun. She wanted to remind him that while he might not think much of her, she was the one with the power at this moment.

"Oh, we have more than that. The man in that house? He isn't dead, and he's pointing fingers." A bit of a bluff might help as well. Owens couldn't know that she wasn't telling the truth. "Gina was trying to get out, so Dinkins lost interest, and he brought her to his friend's house. Next stage..."

"All right, Red. I want to call my lawyer."

"It's Detective Harding. As you wish."

That would give her enough time to clear things with McKenzie and Esposito. So far, so good.

Ellie got up and left the room while Owens was waiting for his attorney.

She found Jordan in the break room, where they could catch their breath before Esposito and McKenzie would arrive. Ellie realized she had avoided the room ever since she'd walked in on Waters and Sam, for no rational reason. She remembered many intense, and sometimes difficult conversations in this room, but it had always felt safe. If she had this reaction, what would it be like for Sam?

The truth was she knew exactly what it was like. Ellie had overcome her visceral reaction to dark places, but she remembered the first days and weeks after her abduction well. Jordan, of course, knew all about those dark places.

"I think it's going okay so far, right?" She knew that Jordan had been watching the interrogation. That still made her a bit nervous because she could remember a time when she'd tried so hard to get noticed, professionally and otherwise. The woman she'd wanted so much had become her wife, but she was also a more experienced detective taking notice of Ellie's performance.

"Yeah, you're doing great." Jordan gave her a warm smile over her coffee, reassuring her. "Damn, there's not enough caffeine in the world to see this through...but if all goes well, maybe we can wrap this up before the dinner party."

Ellie wasn't sure whether she believed they could be so lucky, or if she was just trying to encourage her.

"There will always be loose ends with cases like this," she said.

"Unfortunately, yes. It's a billion-dollar industry. Too many assholes who want their share."

"Well, a few of them won't get it now."

"True." Jordan seemed pensive.

"I know it's not our call, but aren't you kind of glad? I mean...I just think of Brandi, Gina, and everything they did to them."

"I'm not feeling sorry for any of those guys, that's for sure. We still don't know why Dinkins and Oswald were shot with a gun that came from evidence. That part worries me."

"Someone took the law into their own hands?"

"I don't know, but when we walked up the stairs to that house, he had his hands up. He was reaching for something, but that wasn't a gun. We found a couple of handguns and a rifle inside, three shots fired from inside."

"Well, that was enough. Whether he brought any of them outside or not, Torres did have enough reason to shoot him." And secretly, Ellie was glad she had. She wanted whoever was out there with Jordan to have her back. Atwood's words sprang to mind, and she shivered.

"Yes, she did."

"You don't think...?" They knew each other's minds well enough so that Ellie didn't have to finish the question. Or perhaps she wasn't comfortable saying it out loud.

"I think she knows her stuff. And even so, we had no record whatsoever of those two men after they were released from prison. They're dead for five minutes, and Torres is on the scene. It's just...odd."

"It's not like we don't have enough other candidates. This Hank guy had his business up and running, and someone else is coming to town. He doesn't like it, sends a message. Isn't that more likely?"

"I suppose it is."

"But you're not convinced."

"I am convinced we still need to do a ton of grocery shopping before the party. Did Sam get back to you?"

"Yes, she'll be there," Ellie confirmed. "I really hope knowing that she has friends here will help her."

"Atwood still giving you trouble? I know you're doing fine but allow me at least the fantasy of what I might do."

Ellie couldn't help laughing at that.

"What's funny about that? I'd love to put that bigot in his place."

"I think that's what Bristol did already. Chris is giving me dirty looks across the room, but that's all. Bristol has always run a tight ship. He's not going to let one guy screw this up."

"Still, be careful. It only takes one guy."

"I'll be fine. Now if we can get Valerie and McKenzie to agree that Gilbert needs some protection, and Owens' lawyer doesn't mess with us too much, this could be a good day."

Jordan didn't disagree.

◦◦◦

Lieutenant Carroll had advised everyone to help Ellie, should she need it. Jordan thought she was doing an even better job without Waters' interference. She'd always known Ellie was ambitious and eager, but she also had the focus and skills to back it up. It made Jordan irrationally proud to watch her—or perhaps she was entitled to be proud, after finally making good choices in her life.

Still, she knew it wouldn't be easy to make her case to Valerie.

They got a bit of a lucky break an hour later. Jordan and Ellie had retreated to the briefing room with Valerie to bring her up to date when Derek came inside.

"It's on," he said without preamble. "I made contact."

"Did anyone mention Ray?" Esposito asked.

"Oh, it's better than that. The guy I'm meeting with is looking to replace Ray, because he's becoming too chummy with the police. How's that for a bargaining chip?"

"That's awesome," Ellie commented. "Works for me. Counselor?"

Valerie didn't quite share her enthusiasm yet. "Let's see what the lawyer has for us."

<hr>

Jordan stood with Valerie in the observation area while Ellie went to sit across from Owens and his attorney.

"Mr. Owens, I hope you made a decision. There seems to be word on the street that you're talking to the police, so I think it would be best for all of us if we could work together."

She was cool, calm, not giving anything away. Jordan almost envied her. She remembered her early days in an interrogation room, and what it felt like having to keep a façade when there was so much at stake. Push aside the emotions, anger, disgust at what some people were capable of doing to others.

"I want a deal," he said.

"That's not up to me. You have to give us something first."

"What if I can give you the big boss? Will you get me in a witness protection program?"

"Son of a bitch," Valerie muttered.

On the other side of the glass, Ellie asked, "What do you mean by the big boss?"

"Detective, you made it pretty clear that you're interested in the escort service," the attorney explained. "Mr. Owens is ready to give you names of clients, and associates. You could make multiple arrests within the next few hours. I'd say it's in your best interest to get someone from the D.A.'s office in here, and quick."

"Whatever that other guy told you, he's wrong. He's dealing in garbage, and Hank doesn't run garbage."

Jordan felt her stomach churning as she silently translated his words. She was certain Ellie felt the same way. It was something she'd never get entirely used to, Ellie having to be in the same room with low life like that—even if it was part of the job, Ellie's choice.

"You'll have to do a little better than that." Ellie picked up the thread. "Why should we take your word over his? So far, we have him on kidnapping and rape, but you could be charged with murder."

"If you're smart, you'll go with me, and you know it. I can give you everything you want."

There was clearly a different connotation in this. Ellie kept her cool, nonetheless.

"I'll get the A.D.A. Don't waste her time."

Chapter Eleven

"**I**s it okay to feel sick?" Ellie wondered out loud when they left the precinct that night. With the right kind of leverage, Owens' testimony had been proven to be a gold mine for them, though it didn't come for free. In Brandi Gilbert's story, the pieces came together to form the complete picture. Owens had threatened her, coerced her into shooting his boss Robertson. The stress and violence of the situation becoming too overwhelming, she'd been triggered into a state of dissociation that affected her memory, all the while threats from Owens and Hank had been real.

"You didn't give up on her, and now she will finally get help. That's something to be glad about." Jordan touched her shoulder gently before she unlocked the car. "McKenzie is singing your praises, and he's right."

"I don't know. There are so many others. It seems like a bad compromise, depending on where you stand."

"From where I stand, I can see all of them are going down soon. Derek's got a way in, we're going to stage the fake after game party, and that will be it."

"Let's hope so."

They made a stop at the grocery store to buy food for the upcoming party. As they were carrying their bags to the front door, there was a surprise waiting for them.

"Guys," Natalie who sat on the porch steps, said apologetically. "I'm so sorry, but I need to ask you a favor."

⁂

Ellie was on the phone ordering dinner for the three of them, while Jordan put away the groceries.

"This is awkward, right? I am really sorry. I should have never said anything."

Silently, Jordan agreed to everything, but her mind was still on the magnitude of the case, and to some extent, the expanding guest list of their party. For Ellie's sake, and to be pragmatic, she could be forgiving. Natalie would likely be around. She had made a mistake, and they could all move on from that.

"It's okay. I swear."

"I wouldn't have come here if my friend was in town. My apartment is a mess, and so I was hoping you could harbor me until they've taken care of the worst."

"It's not a problem," Jordan said, well aware of her own resistance. She hoped it wasn't showing. It had taken her a long time to be comfortable with friends in close proximity, the person she loved most, even. So, no, she wasn't too happy to share this space with a stranger, but she'd get over it. A few days.

She remembered when they had thought Ariel might come live with them, and the guest room would be hers, but that would have been different.

Natalie was family, though. She'd have to get over herself.

"Dinner will be here in forty-five minutes," Ellie said. "Come on, I'll show you the guest room. There are fresh sheets, towels, and a new toothbrush. If you need anything, let me know."

"I guess then I'll go freshen up." Natalie hugged Ellie and gave Jordan a smile over her shoulder. "This is so kind of you.

It's been a shock—I mean, the landlord is going to pay for it, but I'll still have to clean up."

"I can help you, if you like," Ellie offered.

"Oh no, you don't have to do that. You are so busy, and you're already throwing this party. Once I have an idea what the damage is, and what the landlord is paying for, I'll hire someone to do the rest. If anything, it's a good opportunity for some updates, right?"

If money was not a problem, Jordan wondered, why didn't she just go to a hotel? In fact, there was one located in the Mason tower and the surrounding area where Natalie lived. But that might be just her. Moving in with Kathryn in case of water damage would not have been her first idea.

However, Ellie and Natalie had none of that baggage between them. It might give them a good opportunity to get to know each other better—and Natalie, to avoid any more gross misperceptions in the future.

⟡

"It's a good day. We're moving forward, and someone thought to give me a high-profile assignment," Derek remarked as he put a coffee in front of Jordan and took the lid off of his.

"Yeah. Good for you."

"Come on, you have no reason to be cranky. Case just gained speed, and besides, you got married not long ago."

"Being married is great," she said wistfully. "I'm not cranky. Thanks for the coffee though."

"You seem to be getting along well with Torres? Ellie is doing an excellent job—so what's the problem?"

Jordan hesitated for a few seconds. "Can you keep a secret?"

"It's almost insulting when you make that a question."

"All right. This was supposed to be for the dinner party. We haven't been telling anyone so far, but...Ellie actually has a sister."

"Really? I thought there were no living relatives."

"Yeah, we thought so too, but apparently her father had a child he never new about from an earlier relationship. The mother recently died, and she told her daughter about her father. She did some research and found Ellie."

"Wow." He perched on the edge of her desk. "That's quite the story."

"Almost too good to be true."

"What, you think she's not for real?"

"Well, she hasn't asked for money or run away with the family silver yet." Jordan sighed. "I don't know. The background check came back clean. Ellie's happy. Natalie made quite an impression on her. For such a long time, she thought there was no one, and now..."

"Something's still bothering you," he concluded.

"She had some water damage at her apartment, so now she's going to stay with us for a bit."

Derek chuckled. "I see."

"You see what?"

"Am I wrong to assume this is about...space issues?"

"No, it's not just that. She saw me and Torres at the *Night Shift* and called Ellie to tell her that I might be cheating on her." That still stung. Natalie had no idea about Jordan's past mistakes that could still make her insecure in the present.

"Seems like she got ahead of herself. I think you're not wrong to keep an eye on her. It doesn't sound like she's a criminal mastermind, but I assume that if this doesn't work out, it'd be a big disappointment for Ellie."

"Yeah. Thanks." Jordan took another sip of her coffee. "You're a good partner."

"Don't I know it."

"Carpenter, Henderson. My office."

Neither of them was sure what this was about, but given the lieutenant's serious tone, they followed swiftly. Nina Torres and Ellie were already there, and Carroll tossed the newspaper he was holding onto his desk.

"Please tell me that we'll soon make headlines other than this."

The headline on the front page read – *Sexual Harassment And Bullying In The Police Department. A second accuser has come forward in the case of—*

A bit further down the page, Isabel Combs's mother was quoted.

Why can't they find my daughter?

Derek was meeting with his contact later that night to finalize the details of the after-game party while Jordan spent the time with Nina Torres in a van nearby, listening in. Everything looked and sounded to be on track: The two men Derek was talking to confirmed that as long as the payment was swift, their boss would provide any sort of "entertainment" he wished for. Jordan was certain that the implications were making him just as sick, especially with the other issues surrounding the department at the moment.

The other woman who had accused Waters of harassing her was an officer from the 9th division she had briefly met during another case. This was all happening much too close to home.

"This has to stick," she said. "Otherwise, none of us can justify Owens getting a deal out of it."

"I agree," Nina said. "Well, look at it this way...Oswald and Dinkins didn't get a deal."

"Yeah. Let's hope we'll be able to make some arrests soon and figure out who killed them."

The agent didn't answer to that, so they both went back to listening in. There were two men in the building. They had come in separate cars.

"There's just one problem," Derek said. "How do I know you won't run away with the money? I don't know your boss. You could be trying to rip him off. I need some insurance."

The two men laughed, and there was some rustling. "None of us here has a death wish. As for insurance...boss will give you a chance to sample the merchandise. Here's everything you need to know. Fifty percent now, we get the rest if you're satisfied."

"All right, but again—how do I know you won't rat me out to the cops, and they arrest me the minute I walk through that door?"

"Business wouldn't be what it is if we didn't deliver."

"I suppose. No other bad surprises? I read about the guys who ended up with their brains blown out."

"None of your concern. Take it or leave it."

"No, that's okay. Fifty percent. Anything goes, and you'll clean up afterwards."

"That's the deal."

"I get everything I asked for. That's important. My friends have very specialized tastes. You disappoint them, this is the last time we do business."

"There won't be any problems. Those girls are trained to cater to specialized tastes if you know what I mean. But if you enjoy breaking them in, we can arrange that too."

Jordan caught Nina's glance. Her expression was impassive, but her fingers were clenched in a fist.

"Party favors?" Derek was too experienced to give himself away. Jordan was quite sure the other men didn't even detect that small trace of impatience.

"Sure. Only high quality. Gotta check it all off the list, right? That party will be unforgettable."

"Great. Then we have everything we need," Derek said, the signal for back-up to storm the building. The two men never knew what hit them, and by the time they had a few choice words for the cops, they were already in handcuffs.

"Great job," Torres commented. "It would have been nice to have a confession regarding Dinkins and Oswald."

Derek handed her the folder the men had given him.

"There's something we need to take care of first."

❧

The package included the address of a four-star hotel, and the picture of a woman who looked terrified. Not Isabel Combs. There was a key card as well. The men had warned Derek not to use it right away but knock instead. There was a guard with her who would open the door and wait outside.

"I'm so glad we don't have to deal with these cases on a regular basis," Derek commented as they were on their way. "Give me a cut and dried murder over this any time."

"Yeah. I know what you mean."

"We put away some pretty bad folks. I don't know if it can get lower than that."

Jordan wasn't sure what to say to that—in any case she couldn't come up with anything that might ease his mind.

Once at the hotel, they took the elevator to the eighteenth floor. It made her wonder how they could have set up camp in these surroundings, and if some employee had looked the other way.

Room #322 was at the end of the hall, which was a relief—it potentially made the situation easier to contain. Once they reached the door, Derek knocked firmly.

"It's Henson. I just met with Tripp and Brenner. They said you're expecting me."

Jordan stayed in the background when the man on the other side of the door opened, a knowing grin on his face.

"Come on in, Mr. Henson. We're ready for you. I'm going to step outside and—" He broke off when he found himself face to face with Jordan who was training her gun on him.

"And take a little trip downtown, how about it? You're under arrest..."

They ushered the loudly complaining man back into the suite. Derek stayed with him while officers that had come with them, picked him up. Jordan went into the bedroom.

"It's okay. We're the police. You're safe now."

Her presence barely registered with the naked woman on the bed whose wrists were cuffed to the headboard. Jordan reasoned that she had likely been drugged. In one of the closets, she found a blanket to cover her with, and checking her pulse with one hand, she called for the paramedics to come up.

"You're safe. We're going to get you to a hospital now."

She focused on the woman's pulse under her thumb, making sure her mind wasn't going to slip into a memory or nightmare. In any case, Jordan was grateful that Ellie wasn't here.

Ellie had set up a safe place for Brandi Gilbert, a task much more rewarding than the negotiations with Owens—but both had to be done. Everyone met with the lieutenant for a briefing before the arrested men would be interrogated. She and Nina stood on the other side of the glass while Jordan and Derek went into the room to question Terry Stone, the man who had been guarding the hotel room.

He looked weary, as if he knew that his high-profile boss wasn't likely to send a lawyer for him. In fact, he probably figured that his life was in danger either way. However, he was silent, morosely staring at the investigators.

"You have nothing to say? That's surprising," Derek commented. "It's not like there's an easy way out of this for you. We'll soon arrest more people in your business. I'm sure some of them will be interested in talking to us if they can save their own hide. What's more, a couple of your buddies have already been killed. Someone is not happy with the way your boss does business. None of that worries you?"

"Doesn't look that way," Jordan said. She tossed a couple of pictures on the table, and Ellie noticed the man flinch. "You're going to prison for what you did to that woman in the hotel room either way. The question is what happens afterwards. Or even while you're there. Don't you think the boss has people to watch out for liabilities?"

"I don't know them," he spat, but avoided the photographs.

"So, they weren't working for Hank? You can say that for sure?"

"I didn't say anything. I don't know who did that."

Ellie was startled out of her observations when Nina Torres went to knock on the door and walked inside the room.

"The detective here already explained things to you, and you'd be smart to listen. We want the guy at the top. Honestly? No one cares who shot this low life. Maybe Hank's people, maybe someone else. But we both know folks like him take care of loose ends, so if you don't want to become one of those, you better start talking."

Jordan looked pensive, but she didn't comment on the interruption.

"Let's talk about those after game parties you've been organizing with Owens. Names. Did Isabel Combs ever come up?"

This time, he studied the photograph a bit longer. "Nope, don't know her."

Nina shook her head. "You don't get the gravity of your situation yet." She turned to Jordan. "Come on, let him think about it for a while."

When Ellie drove home, it occurred to her that there was an irony in planning a cheerful party, while at the same time, they were confronted daily with the worst, violence against women, men who treated them like ware, not even human. Men who abused their position of power relative to a female colleague. It made her feel tired and dispirited that they seemed to be working against a tide, and sometimes it was hard to tell if it was finally retreating or still rising. In any case, it brought up many uncomfortable memories.

She hoped Jordan would make it home soon, too, so they could have a quiet rest of the evening.

Ellie couldn't believe her eyes when she walked into the house to find what looked like an elaborate dinner cooking in the kitchen, Natalie greeting her with a smile, a spatula in one hand, a glass of wine in the other.

"Hey, you're home. I hope you don't mind I opened the bottle," she said. "I bought another one. It's almost ready. Is Jordan here, too?"

"No, she had to work longer."

"With the FBI agent?" Natalie asked. Before Ellie could answer, she added quickly, "Forget about it. None of my business. In fact, this is my apology and a thank you for harboring me."

"That's very nice...You didn't have to do that."

"And you didn't have to throw me a party which I admit I'm a bit nervous about but also thrilled...I can't wait to meet your friends. Come, sit down, have a glass." She poured one and handed it to Ellie who was still trying to make sense of the scene.

"This must have taken a while to make."

"I took the afternoon off," Natalie explained. "I had to check on my apartment. I also wanted to make time in case there's anything I can help with for the party. I could take another day."

Frankly, Ellie wished they'd delayed the date for a bit, but everyone was invited now, and she figured it would be helpful to be among people she knew to be good.

"Thank you," she said.

"No problem. It's what family does, right?" With an affectionate smile, Natalie refilled her glass.

Ellie knew she was beyond fortunate, given her family by choice, and this lucky chance. "I want to ask you so many more questions," she mused. "I guess that's not happening today. I'm really tired."

"Don't worry. I'll take care of everything," Natalie promised.

Jordan had listened with mixed emotions when she unlocked the door and heard the laughter from the kitchen. She had to get over herself—after all, Natalie would be back in her own apartment in a matter of days, and they'd go back to their own normal. After a day like this, she selfishly wished she could be alone with Ellie, even knowing how much this new-found relationship with a sister she never knew meant to her.

Her mind was on too many things at once, this situation at home, which was while in no way threatening, still somewhat odd. Nina Torres. She had done nothing that exceeded her competence or jurisdiction. It made sense that her focus might be slightly different, and still... There was something about her that gave Jordan pause. She couldn't put her finger on it.

She finally walked into the kitchen where Ellie and Natalie were sharing a bottle of wine. There wasn't much left in it either.

Ellie got up to embrace her. "You're home!" Jordan couldn't blame her for wanting a little escape. Even though she hadn't been in that hotel room earlier, she surely got the picture.

"Just in time," Natalie added. "I was afraid I'd have to microwave yours, but now we can eat together."

"You didn't have to wait for me, but thanks. It looks great." Her hopes for a quiet evening would not be fulfilled, so she could just as well go with the flow. At least, Natalie produced another bottle of wine.

Jordan had a moment of harrowing guilt thinking of the women they'd found, Gina, locked in a tiny room in a cellar, and Jane Doe, chained to a bed in a hotel room. Isabel Combs was still out there. But they were getting closer, and once they got to the man at the top, they'd be able to topple many others.

She had paid her dues. So had Ellie. Perhaps they deserved to take a moment.

Chapter Twelve

They'd never really had a housewarming party, and not every guest at the wedding had come to their home—so the introduction of Natalie turned out to be the biggest party they'd ever had at their home.

Ellie felt deeply melancholic remembering the dinner parties her parents had loved to host, with friends, family, children...It wasn't quite the same, but close enough to have a pang of grief mixed in with the gratitude that all of these people had accepted their invitation. Derek and Kate had picked up Libby and Sam. Ariel's family hadn't been able to be here, but they had brought her and would come to get her later. She sat with Jack and Pauline. Madeline and her husband had been the closest friends to Ellie's parents. Casey Lyons had come as well, and Darla had brought her toddler.

Family. It could take on so many different meanings. For a brief moment, she wondered if they should have invited Kathryn as well. Jordan had given no indication that she was even thinking about it, so Ellie hadn't pushed the issue.

"I know you're happy everyone's here," she whispered to Ellie. "Now that everyone has their cocktail, perhaps it's time for a few words?"

"Oh my God. I didn't think I'd have to do that."

Natalie had overheard her words. She chuckled. "I'm sorry to say that, but better you than me, sis. You'll do great."

"All right. Let's do this," Ellie mumbled. She found a spoon to clink against her glass.

"Okay…if I could have your attention for a moment. I swear, this won't be long. First of all, thank you all for coming. I'm sure you were wondering what we have to celebrate in the middle of the month, with no holiday near…" Jordan gave her a gentle nudge.

"I have something to celebrate, and I wanted to tell all of you at once. For the longest time, I thought I had no living relative anywhere near. Turns out that's not true, so…I'd like you to meet my sister Natalie," Ellie said, turning to the guest of honor. "Thank you for finding me. Natalie. And thank you all for sharing this moment."

Kate was quickest to make it to her side and hug her. "Ellie, this is amazing!"

"Yeah. I know."

Her friend turned around to shake Natalie's hand. "When did this happen? I can't believe you were able to keep it a secret. Damn. Even Derek kept it a secret from me."

It wasn't a surprise to Ellie that the subject had come up in one of Jordan and Derek's conversations. She didn't mind.

"Natalie came to see me at work." Ellie was aware that Madeline was listening as well, looking pensive.

"My mother told me about my father before she passed away," Natalie said. "I am so grateful she did. I lost her, and I found this wonderful person that is my sister. I'm sorry about the secrecy, but I think we're both still coming to terms with everything."

"I imagine there's a lot to figure out," Madeline said. "When did you say your mother met Patrick?"

"She didn't give me too many details, but it was before Meredith. My mom would have never broken up a family."

Ellie didn't like the challenging tone between the two women, but she trusted both of them to draw the line and not get into a full-blown argument.

"Ellie, can I talk to you for a moment?"

She turned around to face Samantha Potts. "Of course." She went into a somewhat quieter corner with the young officer.

"I wanted to thank you," Sam said. "For everything."

"It's no big deal. You're always welcome. The other day...really, all I did was tell the truth."

"I dreaded coming back to work, but actually, most people were supportive."

"As we should be. You should be able to focus on the job in the first place."

"I try." Sam smiled wistfully. "And congratulations. You must be so happy."

"I am, thank you. I mean it. If there's ever anything you'd like to talk about, you know where to find me."

"I'll remember that," Sam said, then hugged her tightly.

Over her shoulder, Ellie could see that Madeline and her husband were talking to Jack and Pauline now. Natalie stood with Kate and Darla, while Ariel was laughing at something Libby said.

Everything was going according to plan.

Across the room, she caught Jordan's gaze on her, smiling. To be able to share this with her was the best of all.

Family.

⁓

By Monday morning, Natalie had given no indication as to when the pipes in her apartment would be fixed. She was quietly inserting herself into their routines, fixing breakfast and often, dinner during the week. Jordan couldn't bring herself to be critical of the situation, as the game was getting closer, and the men they had arrested during Derek's undercover assignment had enough for them to go up the ladder and meet Hank.

If they were lucky, word wasn't out on their arrest, and they could go directly to him. Many more arrests would follow. There was no room for error or any surprises, so Jordan did something she had put off until now.

Perhaps it was overkill, but she figured it would be better to be safe than sorry. She retreated to the break room and made the call.

"Jordan, what a surprise. I didn't expect to hear from you so soon," the cheerful voice came from the other end of the line."

"A good day to you too."

"Come on, I'm kidding! How are you? Still enjoying married bliss, I hope?"

"It's pretty amazing, but that's not why I'm calling."

"I imagine," Bethany said dryly. "So, what can I do for you?"

"Agent Torres. What's your impression?"

"Smart. Hard-working. Has a great future ahead of her, why do you ask? Are there any problems?"

"No, not really. Just a hunch."

"You have to be a bit more specific."

Jordan suppressed a sigh at the chiding tone. Even though she hadn't talked to her ex in months, some things apparently never changed.

"Okay, here it is. I'm sure you know about the context. We're dealing with some pretty disgusting individuals here, and frankly, it's not hard to wish we could spare the taxpayers some expenses. Of course, none of us would ever go that far."

"What are you saying, that she's on some avenging spree? Come on. Jordan."

"I'm not saying anything, but I have a couple of dead criminals, and a case I can't seem to solve. None of the usual suspects apply. Torres told me herself that she's been working on this for a long time. It's some of the worst I've ever seen. I'm not talking about a spree..."

"But a momentary lapse of judgment? I don't see it."

"We're close to taking down some of the big players, and we still don't know who killed these men. I don't like it."

"I understand, but Torres is clean. You can take my word for it."

"All right then. Thanks."

"You're welcome. You're sure you haven't missed me? No, don't answer that. Say hello to everyone, and good luck."

"Thank you. Bye."

Jordan ended the call, unsure whether she should be relieved, as Maria Doss walked inside after knocking on the door.

"There's someone here for you."

She went back to her desk to find Kathryn sitting in the other chair. Derek and Nina were studying something on his computer screen. If she was lucky, she could do this quick.

"Kathryn. What's up? I'm sorry, I don't have much time."

"You never do. I just wanted to see how you're doing."

"I'm good. You?"

She saw that Nina had gotten up and was waiting at a respectful distance.

"I'm doing okay...and I wanted to know if we could meet again. The way it was before."

"Can we talk about this another time? This is really not the moment..."

"Will you pick up the phone?"

"Yes. Give it a few days, please."

"I hope you had a nice party this weekend," Kathryn said, then she turned to walk away. Jordan resisted the urge to follow her. There was no reason. She'd talk to her when she had the time...and find out how she could know about the party in the first place. She must have driven by the house. The fact that she hadn't come in struck Jordan as unusual. Perhaps she was finally demonstrating respect for boundaries, though her disappointed tone said otherwise.

⁂

The next few days were spent with tense preparations at work. Natalie had several conversations with her landlord, discovering that there was more need for renovations than she had imagined. She was still cooking the occasional meal.

"I am so sorry. I didn't think it would take that long. If I could stay until the weekend? If it's not fixed after that, I'll go to a hotel, I promise. Would that be okay?"

"Of course," Jordan said at the same time as Ellie offered, "Stay as long as you need."

Jordan didn't mention it on the way to work, so Ellie assumed either solution would be fine. She, too, had at first wondered why Natalie had chosen to stay with them, but she had to admit it was fairly comfortable.

As it was, they had many other things to consider at the moment: They had intercepted a conversation between an associate of the men Derek had met with, and someone they believed to be Hank.

Nina had called in reinforcements. Hank was going to see a couple of "business" partners, and make sure everything was going to happen to his customers' satisfaction. In the conversation, the names of a judge and a politician were mentioned. Both had rented spaces for private parties afterwards, but if all went well, they'd get to them—and Hank—before.

There would be uniformed officers at the game as usual, but this time, there was a lot more to look out for. Nina had mentioned that Isabel Combs might not even be in the state, or the country, any longer, but Ellie didn't want to give up hope just yet. She was beyond thrilled to have her own part in the briefing during roll call, remembering when she'd been on the other side, casting longing glances whenever it was Jordan joining Sergeant Bristol in the room. She had everything she wanted, and so much more.

Ellie hoped they'd be able to help many who weren't so lucky in one fell swoop with this operation.

"Remember, those clients are important to him. He will likely check in with both of them, and when he does, we need to act right away. Thank you."

Casey came by, patting her shoulder. "You don't miss being on the other side?"

"I am grateful for every minute of it," Ellie said. "But no, I love being where I am. Let's get this guy."

"Absolutely. And Ellie...I wanted to tell you thanks. You did a great job with Potts."

Ellie shrugged. "It's the normal thing to do, right? You guys came through for me when I needed people I could trust. I hope she'll find the same thing here."

"Me too," Casey agreed. "I'll see you later. Good luck."

"Good luck to us."

⁂

They had a bit of time before they had to leave for the stadium, so Jordan offered to do a quick coffee run. It was sheer coincidence that she stopped behind a familiar car at a red light: Natalie's. The party had been a success, and frankly, that had been a relief for Jordan. The people that had accepted their invitation were neither paranoid nor naïve, and all of them had welcomed Natalie. As much as Jordan valued her space, she couldn't argue much with all those recent home-cooked meals either. Madeline was the only one who remained cautious, but she'd been a close friend of Ellie's mother, so that was only natural, right?

Jordan drove past the coffee shop and stayed behind Natalie, keeping enough of a distance so the latter wouldn't know she was being followed. She wasn't sure what she hoped to learn from this, but instinct told her this might be the best opportunity she'd get. Fortunately, Natalie stopped a few blocks later and parked on the curb in front of an apartment building. Jordan slowed down the car and found herself a spot three cars behind her. She was lucky: A woman came out with a couple of bags. Jordan held the front door open for her and slipped inside. She could still hear footsteps on the stairs, so she followed silently. Natalie stopped on the second floor, where she went to an apartment near the staircase, and opened the door with a key. The name on the sign said "Douglas." Who was that person?

This was not where Natalie had told them she lived, the building with the water damage. Why make up a story like this? Jordan checked her watch, wishing she didn't have to be somewhere within the next hour. She couldn't confront Natalie right now, but she would get answers. Jordan found this disconcerting. She didn't have much of a choice, and at least Ellie would be at work too.

Natalie's secrets might be completely harmless, and for Ellie's sake, Jordan hoped that they were. There was no doubt Natalie could be charming, and she had made herself a tolerable house guest...still. If she had another apartment, why hide the fact? Why rent it under a different name? There was a Natalie Morgan living in the building currently undergoing renovations. She was working in an office at the Mason tower, and her car registration was for the vehicle Natalie drove. What piece was she missing?

The ringing of her cell phone made her jump, and she quickly stepped away from the door.

"Everyone's wondering where that coffee is," Derek said. "You went to get those beans in Guatemala or what?"

"On my way," she assured him. "Sorry about that."

"Is everything okay?"

"Yeah. It's just taking a moment."

"All right. See you soon—I hope."

Jordan took another look at the door and turned to leave. In her car, she called a detective in another division.

"Let me guess," April said. "You need a favor."

Jordan sighed. "You know me so well."

If she hurried now, she'd still bring the coffee in time before everyone would leave.

Chapter Thirteen

J ordan still sat at her desk, absent-mindedly sipping her coffee. Ellie couldn't help but worry. First the coffee run that seemed to have taken a lot longer than necessary, and then she had looked up something but minimized what was on the screen the moment Ellie arrived. Perhaps she was focused, ahead of this all-important assignment, but Ellie wanted to be sure.

"Is something wrong?" she asked.

"No, I don't think so. I just had to check something. What about you? You're all ready?"

"I so am. A lot of people have been waiting for this day."

"I'm sure Ms. Gilbert is very grateful for everything you did. You never gave up on her."

"Well, yeah, Waters shouldn't have either. He was primary on the case, and...now I wonder if there might have been others, especially in the past year. He seemed really eager to get out."

"Oh, don't say that." Maria Doss sighed. "That could mean IA will look at all of his cases, and some of them were mine too. This is going to take a while either way."

"You're right about that," Jordan said as she got up and picked up her keys. "But now we have other things to worry about."

Ellie couldn't help it—she still thought Jordan's tone might be revealing she was occupied with something in addition to the case. She didn't want to address this in front of Maria. Perhaps Kathryn had decided that the break in communication was too long for her. She was going to ask again after tonight.

Ellie's first task at the stadium was to intervene in a fight between fans, though when she arrived at the scene, the two opponents didn't present a problem any longer. Instead, it was Chris Atwood yelling at this colleague, Sam Potts.

"Don't tell me what to do! You can be grateful this department has a thing for minorities, otherwise it would be you out of a job."

"Chris. Hey. What's the problem?"

Silently, Ellie questioned the wisdom of putting Atwood and Potts this close together. She had no doubts which of the two had started the argument.

"She's supposed to cover this section."

"I did. There were two groups of fans arguing. One threw a cup, and they went at each other...I needed some help."

"That sounds reasonable to me. Was there any trouble in your section too?" Ellie asked even though she was fairly certain she knew the answer already.

"You're not my boss," he spat, turned, and walked away.

"Everything okay on your end?" she asked Sam, who nodded, her frustration obvious. Perhaps she should have a word with Bristol at the end of the day. So far, Atwood had only been a nuisance, but that might change.

She wasn't here to keep the peace between fans of opposing teams. So far, only the politician had shown up with a group of aides and security personnel.

Neither the judge nor the elusive Hank had shown their faces yet. The politician wouldn't be so brazen with this many people around? Or were some of them in on it? Owens had provided young women for Robertson. Nothing was impossible when people were greedy and ruthless.

She hoped that for many of them, luck would run out tonight. Ellie went back to her post, where she took a moment to contact Casey Lyons. "Do me a favor and keep an eye on Atwood and Sam, okay?"

"You don't even have to ask," her friend said.

The judge eventually showed up in his VIP box, together with a much younger woman that was neither his wife, nor one of the trafficked women they were on the lookout for. They learned that she was a secretary from his office.

Nina Torres groaned. "That leaves us with nothing much on him, and he certainly knows how far we can go with that. I want to bring him in anyway. Maybe she knows something as well. His name was on that tape, damn it."

Jordan agreed whole-heartedly with that assessment. Hank's clients were in high profile positions—that also made it harder to get to them. That tape helped, but they needed more than that.

"Ellie? Derek?" she asked via the two-way radio.

"Everything is quiet here," Derek assured her from the other side of the VIP lounge. "Wait, one of his aides just left. Let's see what he's up to."

A few tense moments passed, before he reported back: "That would be hot dogs."

About ten minutes passed before the judge's companion left her seat as well. The game had begun. The noise level in the stadium was rising.

Another ten minutes passed, then twenty, but the woman didn't come back. Then two men joined the judge in the VIP box, one of them tall and broad-shouldered, the other one shorter, wearing a suit and bleached blonde hair: Hank.

"Bingo," Nina said. "Henderson, Harding, don't let your guy get further than the parking garage. We're on the move."

Jordan briefly thought she would have preferred if they could have gotten to them somewhere further away from the crowd, and she hoped no shots would be necessary. The last thing anybody needed was a mass panic.

❧

The politician and his security staff were getting ready to leave, even though the game was barely into the second quarter.

Ellie and Derek unobtrusively followed until one of the guards spun around and held up his hand. "Stay back! You can't go this way."

"Oh, I'm sure we can," Derek said, holding up his badge. "Detective Henderson, this is Detective Harding. Mr. Cornell, we have a few questions regarding..."

They'd seen this many times from a suspect during an impending arrest, but neither of them had expected the State Representative hopeful to run.

"Are you kidding me?" Derek asked to no one, while Ellie gave chase.

"Suspect is trying to escape, now Block 82B. Can anyone see him?"

It was the worst possible moment for a touchdown, nearly everyone in the stadium on their feet.

"We're close," Casey answered via the radio. "Atwood, Potts?"

"Ellie, are you anywhere close?" Officer Potts asked. "We got him. 82 B, row 25."

"Great. I'll be right there." Ellie hastened down the steps and a moment later, she saw Sam and a male officer, the angry-looking man with them in handcuffs.

"I have no idea what this is," he snapped, "but you're going to pay for it. I have done nothing wrong. I'm going to sue you, and your boss, and every single one of you."

Casey arrived as well. Ignoring the rather empty threats, Ellie asked, "Where is Atwood?"

"Geez, Harding, why do you have to be such a bitch all the time..." He broke off when he realized that Casey, and now Derek, were with them.

"Good," she said. "Why don't we take this elsewhere and let the folks enjoy the game?"

<hr>

At the precinct, Ellie and Derek went to interrogate Cornell while Jordan and Nina sat down with the main suspect Henry Maddows a.k.a Hank. He was much too comfortable for a man who would be charged on multiple counts of human trafficking, abuse, torture, and possibly, murder.

"My clients come from all over the world. I provide high class entertainment to them, and yes, I run a legal escort service." Hank leaned back in his chair. "I assume my lawyers will soon sort all of this out."

"Once they've sorted through the numerous charges against you, sure," Jordan said.

"Oh honey. I've been over this with the cops before. None of that will stick."

Nina slammed the folder onto the table with such vehemence even he flinched.

"In the past, that might have been true, but you got a little careless. We have sworn testimonies from a number of witnesses who either made money with you or made you money. Too bad for you that some folks got greedy, and one of your high-profile clients was killed."

"Speaking of lawyers, I'd like my phone call now, before you ladies embarrass yourselves even more."

"You can call him in a moment. Detective Carpenter, could you give us a minute?"

Jordan hadn't expected anything like this so early in the interrogation, and so far, he hadn't given them any clue as to the original murder case. Nina had to know what she was doing.

From the other side of the window, she watched with Lieutenant Carroll as Nina continued, "Look, I've been doing this for a long time. Let's stop pretending we don't know exactly what this is about. I'll have my colleagues turn off the cameras, so it's just the two of us." She leaned closer, whispering something.

There was another agent watching with them, one of the additional personnel Nina had asked for. "Let's turn off those cameras," he said.

"This is highly unusual." Carroll wasn't amused, but he didn't have much of a choice.

The body language of the two people in the interrogation room was intriguing, and, to some extent, surprising. The man sitting in that chair treated women as commodity—for sure, there was no respect whatsoever from his side. Still, Agent Torres dominated the scene, and whatever it was she was telling him at the moment, seemed to cut through his cocky attitude.

Given her own initial suspicions, and Bethany's reaction to them, Jordan was beyond curious. She took a second to check her cell phone, noticing that there were no new messages. Good.

If April thought there was an emergency, she would have contacted her right away.

As if on cue, there was a knock on the door, and Ellie walked inside.

"Our guy has realized that he won't be winning any elections anytime soon, but he's willing to work with us as long as we don't tell his wife he booked Hank's services, not that she won't find out when he goes to prison." She looked disgusted but kept her tone level and professional. "He has some documentation, and texts. There'll be a lot of evidence to go through."

"Thanks, Harding," the lieutenant said. "See Bristol and have a couple of uniforms help you with that."

"Will do. How's it going here?"

That was also meant for Jordan who was guiltily reminded of secrets she was keeping from Ellie. Once they were able to leave here, she would confess.

"So far, so good."

"Big day," Sergeant Bristol commented when Ellie found him in his office.

"Oh yes, and it seems there is no end to it yet. I was hoping I could borrow Martin and Potts?"

"No objections from me. What happened with Atwood?"

Ellie hesitated a split-second. Then again, she already had a reputation with Atwood and his friends. It wasn't like she was setting him up to fail. Just like his friend Cliff Waters, he was doing a fine job himself.

"From what I know, Potts needed help with some fans going at one another. He was biding his time. He and Detective Waters were friends, but that's no excuse."

"I agree."

"Potts, on the other hand, caught a suspect. She did a great job."

"So, you're rewarding her by having her sift through a ton of papers." Bristol chuckled when Ellie opened her mouth to protest. "Don't worry, I don't think she'll mind. I remember another officer who was eager for every minute she could spend with Homicide."

Ellie hoped she wasn't blushing too hard.

"I hear you've been doing a great job as well these past months. Congratulations."

"Thank you, Sergeant. I'm grateful for all the opportunities I had. If you'll excuse me now..."

"Of course, Detective."

As she left the office, Ellie felt a little taller. All of her dreams had come true. The most urgent ones, anyway. There might be a few left, but there was time. First of all, they had to get the documents in question and go through all of them.

⁂

When Thalia left her apartment, one of her neighbors came out of his at the same time, and they walked to the stairwell together.

"Hey, how are you?" she asked.

He smiled back at her.

"Great. Even better if you introduce me to your friend sometime."

Thalia frowned. "Which friend are you talking about?"

"The one who was at your door earlier? Tall, brunette?"

"Oh. Yes, of course. I'm sure she'd be happy to meet you." She halted abruptly. "Damn, I forgot something. See you later."

"Sure. Have a great day."

"You too."

She headed back to her apartment and walked inside the guest room. The sight never failed to make her smile.

Chapter Fourteen

All of their shifts had long overlapped with the night shift, and by the time they made it to the likewise named bar, it was well after nine. Nina Torres would leave town soon, so this would be the last chance for Jordan to find out whatever it was she had said to Hank in the interrogation room.

She had the feeling that not every single word would be in Nina's report, and the man in question was now in federal custody. Still no news as to who had killed Dinkins and Oswald, but some of Hank's properties had been raided, more associates arrested, and more women freed. It was a good day...though there were still missing pieces to it. On Torres' end. And regarding another issue. Ellie had texted Natalie that they wouldn't be home for dinner. Natalie wished them good luck and said she was going to spend the evening on the couch with TV and a glass of wine. Thumbs up emoji.

April hadn't gotten back to Jordan, and she assumed it wouldn't happen before the next day. There might be a perfectly normal explanation. Either way, she was going to find it. Above everything, Ellie deserved the truth.

Maria Doss had joined them as well, sulking a bit because she couldn't be at the game.

"Who was playing anyway?" Jordan asked, making everyone crack up with laughter.

"What kind of lesbian are you?"

"Really? That was work, and of course I know who played. I just couldn't care less. Everything else is for my wife to judge." Her words led to more amusement in the group, and a pensive look from Nina Torres. Ellie looked content with herself and the world. Jordan hoped she wouldn't have to put a damper on her good mood soon.

One thing at a time.

She waited until some members of their group had gone to get some drinks. Ellie had briefly taken a seat at another table with Sam, Libby Marshall, and a couple of other officers.

"Quick," Nina Torres joked. "What do you want to know?"

"Am I that transparent?"

"Actually, no. I wouldn't have known if I hadn't talked to Dr. Roberts."

"Oh. Right." *Thanks, Bethany.*

"She was right to tell me, you know. But you should have come to me first."

In the context of this conversation, after the multiple arrests of this day, there was an awkwardness to the subject, even more so when Jordan remembered Natalie's suspicions.

"Yeah, I should have. Forget about it. I'm sorry."

"No need. I did shoot that guy to save my ass and yours. Would I have liked to do it anyway? Of course. Have I thought about it a million times? Absolutely. But we need as many of those scumbags alive so we can help the women."

"I understand that. Really, I'm sorry. I don't know why—"

"I know. Perhaps you sensed something about me that bothered you."

"Nina..." At this point, Jordan was fairly concerned about how much Bethany might have told her. "I don't think we need to have this conversation. I made a mistake."

"That depends. Look, things could have gone either way for me. I assume you understand about having a crappy childhood."

This was going in a completely different direction from what she had anticipated. So much for instincts.

"I do, but I'm still here." Kathryn had committed to change in the past few years. Jordan didn't feel she needed to give her much credit for her parental skills in her early years.

"Yeah, so am I, even though my foster parents found it convenient to make money off me. I'm glad to have this job. There are rules. They actually keep my desire to kill in check. I'm kidding," she added when the alarm must have shown on Jordan's face. "About the killing part, anyway. The rest is unfortunately true."

"I'm sorry. My mother, she wasn't like that. She just..." Was too high and drunk most of the time to realize what was going on around her? She and her husband had barely noticed when a grown man gave their twelve-year-old daughter drugs. "I guess it could have been worse."

"There's always worse, but it's not a competition. Something tells me that there's no need to defend her."

"Something or someone?"

Nina shook her head. "Bethany told me that you two were in a relationship once. That's all. I didn't ask for details, and the rest was only about the case. I swear."

"How did you get out?"

"Not every single person in the world sucks, that's how. I was lucky to have some good people support me."

"Did you ever see your foster parents after that?"

"I didn't have to. They were killed in a shooting...police suspected a drug deal gone bad, and given my memory of them, I don't have any reason to doubt that."

Jordan had the sudden impulse to go see Jack and Pauline and hug them tightly. Given the time of night, she resisted—and besides, this wasn't the only uncomfortable conversation waiting for her.

"If at some point, you get Hank to spill who killed Oswald and Dinkins, let me know," she said. "Just so I can close that file."

"Sure. I'll let you know."

"Thanks."

"No problem. But after getting all of those confessions out of me, I think you owe me, Detective. Let's have those shots."

Jordan wasn't going to dispute the suggestion.

⁓

When Ellie returned to their table, Jordan took her aside, deciding she could no longer wait.

"Okay, what's the plan?" Ellie asked, amused and unaware. She leaned in for a kiss. "If you were looking for privacy, how about we go home?"

"Ellie. Hold on a second."

"That sounds serious."

"I'm afraid it is. It's about Natalie."

Ellie's eyes widened. "Is she okay? What happened?"

"She's fine," Jordan hastened to assure her, chastising herself. The last time someone had to break bad news regarding family to Ellie, it had been about her parents. "Remember, earlier, when I was getting coffee?"

"Which took you forever."

"Yeah. That's because I followed her."

"Jordan. Come on. I thought we were past this." Ellie turned away, clearly frustrated with the turn of events. "I know she got some things wrong, but she apologized. Multiple times."

"That's not what this is about. She went to another apartment, not the one with the water damage. She has the keys. I don't mind her living with us, but she said it's because of the renovations. What is that other place for?"

"I have no idea. It could be harmless."

"Sure. I hope it is."

Ellie turned to her with a resigned expression, her shoulders slightly slumped.

"There's more, isn't there?"

"I don't know yet. There's another name on the door, and I asked April to look into it."

"Fraud? We have the background check. Nothing came up."

"Because we didn't have that other name."

"She had a picture. That was real!" Ellie was beginning to understand what this could mean. Her desperate tone broke Jordan's heart.

"I'm so sorry. April hasn't gotten back to me yet...So I guess we have to wait." Jordan drew her into an embrace, but Ellie stepped back from it.

"No, we don't have to. Let's go home and clear this up right now. I'm sure she'll have an explanation."

"Ellie, please, why don't we—"

"I'm not mad at you. I swear. I probably would have done the same thing, and...I need to know. Right now."

"Okay then. Let's get a cab."

It was the second time in as many conversations that Jordan felt her own family situation was relative to the challenges of others. But this was different. This was about Ellie. If Natalie had set out to hurt her, there would be hell to pay.

⁂

In the past few weeks, Natalie had become a reliable presence. Of course, they hadn't grown up together, so the process was a different one. Ellie appreciated talking to her, about their jobs, their parents, the dreams they'd had and the ones they still harbored for the future.

A second apartment—what could that mean? Maybe nothing. Jordan's friend hadn't turned up anything. It would all be fine. They'd talk about it and leave it behind them. It made so much sense that Jordan's experiences had made her extremely cautious about a family member turning up out of the blue. Regarding Kathryn, she had been right to be cautious. This was different, wasn't it?

Come to think of it, Natalie had asked a lot of questions, more than she'd answered. Modesty—or did she have something to hide?

"You know I want to be wrong."

Jordan hadn't said much else during the cab ride.

Ellie believed her. "Yes, I know." She looked down at their joined hands. "Perhaps we are just paranoid. We got somewhat of a reason to be paranoid, right?"

"Yeah. Now let's go wake your sister and totally annoy her."

Neither of them felt much humor in that statement, but Ellie was determined to cling to hope until proven otherwise. Inside the house, she walked right up to the guest room.

"Natalie?"

"Ellie!" Jordan called from the living room downstairs. "Come here for a moment."

She childishly wished she could simply stay where she was and avoid seeing what Jordan wanted to show her. That impulse only lasted a few seconds. Ellie couldn't have made it to where she was by running from the truth. Maybe Natalie wasn't a perfect person, but she was still her sister. They'd figure something out. Maybe she needed help.

Ellie walked into the living room, instantly reminded of the text message she'd gotten earlier. On the table sat an open bottle of wine and a half-filled glass. An envelope with her name on it was leaning against the bottle, and the TV was on. It was just the scene Natalie had described—save for the envelope.

"Why do I have the feeling I should put on gloves for that?" she wondered out loud. Whatever it was, she wasn't going to let disappointment crush her. Not on a day like this when she'd been once more reminded that so many people—so many women—had it much worse. Her concerns paled in comparison.

Ellie finally reached out to open the envelope. Inside was a typed letter, and Ellie's debit card.

I hate goodbyes, so let me tell you this way. I really enjoyed my time with you. You two are adorable. From there, it went downhill quickly. *Thanks for being a real challenge—I knew that at least one of you would insist on a background check early on. Hey, you tried, but I've been doing this for a while. Ellie, I'm sorry I had to borrow a few things from you. Anyone would be happy to have you as a sister. I almost wish it was true. Have a great life, and don't waste your time trying to find me. Everyone has failed. N.*

Ellie looked up from the paper, too stunned to react at all, as if someone had knocked the wind out of her. Once she started to breathe again, the pain would hit her.

"Ellie. Sit for a second."

"No. There's no time. Where did you say that apartment was?" Ellie rushed to take her coat and purse from the coat rack. "Send a unit," she said. "I don't think it's likely, but maybe we can still catch her. We need a BOLO—you remember the license plate number? I want to go to the apartment myself, the one where you saw her and the one with the water damage."

"Is there anything else I can do?" Jordan asked softly.

"Not right now." Ellie still couldn't allow the hug. She knew that if she did, she might start crying, and she couldn't give in to her emotions right now. There was no doubt Natalie had done this to others. They had to catch her. "I need to be a cop right now, before anything else. And I need you to do the same."

"Of course. I'm sorry."

"I know. Let's make sure she doesn't get away with this."

Ellie was holding up. Jordan suspected that it was the number of practical things to do that saved her at the moment. She felt irrationally guilty for bringing up the subject in the first place—but the facts didn't change. That way, Ellie had at least a small heads-up, though it was still an incredible blow.

Finally, there was a text message from April who apologized for not getting back to Jordan earlier.

I found something. Call me. Jordan called her right back.

"Hey, I'm sorry," April said. "I was swamped here. I'm looking at these records now, and Douglas is an elderly gentleman who died a couple months ago. There's no record of a new tenant."

"She's gone. We're on our way to the apartment now."

"Damn it!"

"It's not your fault. Everyone was swamped yesterday."

"Yeah, but now it's my business. I'll let you know if I find anything else. You do the same?"

"Sure." Jordan ended the call, looking over at Ellie who had been silent from the moment they got into the car. She was focused on the road. Jordan barely stopped herself from saying she was sorry, again. "We'll find her."

"Yeah."

They both knew it wouldn't be much of a consolation for Ellie.

Chapter Fifteen

T he apartment was empty, like no one had lived there for some time. The only reminder of who had had the keys recently was an article cut out from a newspaper: *Local Hero*, written by a reporter named Allen. Ellie had saved a woman from a burning vehicle that day.

Natalie might have forgotten the article. More likely, she had strategically placed it on the floor, so they'd find it the moment they came in. The more time passed, the clearer Ellie could see what had happened, and how she'd let herself be tricked. Natalie had invaded every aspect of her life. She had tried to turn her against Jordan.

"Oh God. I gave a speech to all our friends and introduced her as my sister." She felt sick at the memory, their friends' innocent reactions to her happiness. How could anyone have known? Natalie was a pro. But Madeline had been suspicious.

"None of this was your fault," Jordan said firmly.

"I used that debit card once in her presence when we met at the restaurant. She must have gotten the pin number then and stolen it from my purse later. How did she even do that?"

"We'll figure it out once we find her. There must be people in this building that interacted with her. Let's find out." Determined, she walked over to the door on the other side of the hallway and knocked, regardless of the fact that it was past midnight.

"Police! Open the door!" It took another round of knocking before the door was opened a small fraction, and a man in his late twenties, wearing only boxer shorts, peeked outside. His eyes widened when he saw Jordan's badge.

"Oh shit, you're for real," he said.

"Can we talk?" Jordan asked, and he removed the chain.

"Sure, just let me get a shirt." He was back a moment later, studying her curiously. "Is something wrong? I was joking to Thalia about introducing me, but I didn't think you'd be back so soon."

"Thalia." Ellie suppressed a groan. Chances were this wasn't Natalie's real name either.

"Your neighbor across the hall?"

"Yes, she moved in a few months ago, I think. I saw her in the hallway sometimes. What did she do?"

"Do you know where she is? Did she mention anything to you, her work, places she went?"

He ran a hand through his hair.

"No, I don't think so. We...flirted a little. I have a thing for older women, you know."

Jordan didn't roll her eyes at him, but Ellie was certain she wanted to.

"If you can think of anything, please let us know," she said, handing him a card. "It's important that we find her."

***

Sometimes, Jordan had fantasized about the relationship she might have with Kathryn in the present. The attempt was usually marred by a memory. She was aware that Ellie's situation differed greatly—nothing about Natalie had been real. Her efforts to connect, her affection, the family photos, everything was fake.

It was stunning how Natalie had inserted herself into their lives, and they had let her, because...It seemed like such a miracle for Ellie to find her only living relative. Both of them had wanted it to be true. She assumed that exploiting her victim's hopes was part of Natalie's M.O. Ellie still hadn't said much, but her posture revealed a sadness that was staggering. When they finally got home, Jordan wanted nothing but to hold her, shut out the world for a moment. To her relief, Ellie didn't resist when they were in bed together.

"If you want to talk..."

"I'm sorry. I just want to sleep. Tomorrow will be a long day."

"Yeah." Jordan kissed her softly and tightened her embrace. It was all she could do at the moment. Tomorrow was another story.

It was earlier than she would have liked when her phone rang. Jordan reluctantly reached for it and answered. Ellie hadn't stirred. "Carpenter."

"Jordan, you need to see this," Derek said. "Remember Stone, the guy we arrested at the hotel? He made bail, but he's not going to make it to trial."

Jordan pushed back the covers and reached for her jeans. "What happened?"

"One shot to the head."

"Your timing sucks."

"Hey, don't blame me. I didn't shoot him...Though there was a moment..."

"Yeah." Jordan hadn't forgotten anything about that hotel room and the woman shackled to the bed. "Where are you?"

"On the scene." Derek gave her the address. "If you could get here sometime in the near future...?"

"Yeah, I'll be there as soon as I can." Leaving Ellie alone was the last thing she wanted to do at the moment, but perhaps she could get a little more rest before her own shift.

"What's going on?"

"You can go back to sleep for a bit."

"Is this about Natalie?"

"No. Apparently another one of the traffickers was shot, after he made bail. I'll meet Derek at the scene."

"Okay," Ellie mumbled, and pulled the covers back up to her chin.

"Take it easy today. April and her colleagues are on the case now. They're going to find her."

"Sure."

Jordan sat on the edge of the bed, leaned over, and kissed her. "You'll be okay. I'll see you later. I love you."

⁂

When the alarm rang, Ellie got out of bed, went into the shower, and got dressed, like every morning. In the past few days, they'd often woken to the scents of coffee and breakfast foods.

Jordan had put coffee and water into the coffeemaker before she left, and while it was brewing, Ellie reflected on the past few days. It was a relief that she didn't feel like crying much—perhaps the urge would vanish altogether.

"How crazy are you, doing all that cooking," she said out loud. What now? Another party, another speech, gather everybody and tell them it was all a hoax? What had been Natalie's goal anyway, other than the about $2000 she had spent on various items in the past twenty-four hours? She had also taken a couple of dresses, a skirt and a couple of tops from Ellie's side of the closet. Was she up to something more sinister? Or did she simply enjoy fooling people into believing her? Something didn't add up. Ellie wasn't too thrilled about the money. The way Natalie had made herself a part of the story, her story and that of her family, was even more disturbing to her. And she'd been alone in the house, likely opening more doors than that of the pantry. They kept important documents in a safe, sure, but even so, this was their home, their life on display for everyone.

And Ellie had invited her in.

But the background check had come back clean. She, they, weren't that naïve.

Ellie poured herself a cup of coffee.

There had hardly been a day when she felt less like going to work, and for a moment, she thought about calling Kate and starting the day with alcohol and avoiding everyone else.

But she didn't...because then she'd have to tell her friend the real reason.

The world didn't stop, and there were still people who had it worse than her, people who needed her. She wasn't going to let them down.

⸺⸻⸺

"You said something about timing," Derek reminded her. "Long night?"

He had only briefly joined them at the *Night Shift* the other night but then left to meet Kate McCarthy, Jordan remembered. They would all find out anyway, so maybe it would be helpful if they knew in advance.

"Natalie's gone," she said. "Wrote some crazy letter, withdrew the maximum amount with Ellie's debit card, and raided her closet. It's bizarre."

"You're kidding me?"

She gave him a long look. "You really think I'd make up something like that?"

"No, of course not. Damn, that's bad. How's Ellie?"

"Okay, considering. Actually...I'm not sure. We did everything we could, now our friends over in Fraud are taking care of this."

"Damn."

"You said that already."

"It bears repeating."

Jordan couldn't argue with that. "So, what did I miss?"

"I'm so glad you're interested." Dr. Adams looked up from where she was crouching next to the body. "Obviously, this looks familiar. Same precise execution."

"Someone wants us to know they've done this before, I assume," Jordan said.

"A self-appointed avenger, or someone whose job it is to get rid of witnesses," Derek agreed. "Either way, we should check in with Esposito. A few of those guys will be tried here, and some of them know about Hank. We want them to be able to testify."

"I'll do that," she said, taking a look around the apartment. It looked like a carbon copy of the one where they had found Dinkins and Oswald. "How about I go right now? I'll need to check something else as well."

"Tell Ellie I'm really sorry. If I can do anything..."

"Thanks. We'll let you know."

❦

Ellie sat at her desk, thinking back to when Natalie had first come here. It was now clear to her that she must have done her homework meticulously. She already knew that Ellie and Jordan would check on her some, but also that they had busy lives, with long work hours.

She had known about Ellie's grief and woven a story around it. Chances were Natalie's mother was well and alive. She swiped through her phone, pictures taken at the party, and realized that Natalie had never directly looked into the camera.

"Ellie, hi."

Sam Potts, carrying two cups of coffee, startled her out of her thoughts. "Hey. I was taking a break from the files. I thought after the day we all had yesterday, you could use one."

Ellie gratefully accepted the steaming cup. She wondered how her troubles compared to Sam's, if they did, in any way.

Besides...She had been attacked, taken from her home once. They had dealt with a serial killer's fixation with Jordan. This, in comparison, was nothing. Why did it freak her out so much? She could give herself the answer. Natalie had messed with her mind, the memories of her parents, the memories Meredith and Patrick's friends had of them.

"Sit for a moment," she said.

"Thanks."

Of course, this had to be the moment Atwood walked through the room, giving both of them a glare. Instead of him, Ellie had assigned Wes Martin, who had been in her class at the academy.

"How are you holding up?" Ellie asked.

"I'm better. Work is my saving grace."

"Yeah. I know how that feels. Look, Sam..."

The young officer listened attentively. Ellie realized all of a sudden that while she'd likely have to face the subject many more times, she couldn't tell her, not now. There was a surprising amount of shame attached to it. She knew they had done everything possible, even more so than any civilian person could have done if an alleged long-lost relative showed up. Natalie had taken money, but judging from the amount of it, that might not have been her main motivation. She enjoyed the manipulation.

What else was there that they might not know about?

"Keep up the great work," she said. "Did you find anything interesting yet in those documents?"

⁓

Somehow, Ellie made it through the day, and they met at the *D&T* with Kate and Derek. Jordan didn't have any new information other than a detective in Fraud was on the case and would inform them as soon as they had any leads.

"I'm really sorry," Kate said, her gaze somber as she hugged Ellie. "Makes me wish I was still working with you, and I could help you find the bitch."

"We'll do what we can to make that happen," Derek assured. "What are you having? I'll pay."

"I can't pass up that chance." Ellie hoped that a few drinks would at least keep the deep sadness away for a few hours. At times, it drowned out the bitter self-reproach that she should have known better. She had also pushed every single doubt aside because she'd been so happy to have found family, something that was no longer true. But the things she and Jordan had told Ariel about chosen family still were. "Jordan will drive. Since she had shots with Torres the other day, it's only fair."

She caught Jordan's glance on her, both affectionate and concerned. Being with her was a safe space that Natalie hadn't been able to invade. At the moment, it might be the only thing that kept her sane.

Chapter Sixteen

Ellie's plan might have been to get drunk, and Jordan would have made sure she could do so safely, but to her relief it didn't come to that. They talked about work, Kate's pre-law classes and plans for the near future. James McKenzie came by with his husband and stopped at their table briefly, the conversation lifting Ellie's spirits. She had achieved a lot in little time. Jordan knew she'd refuse to let anything keep her down, though this was a tough case indeed. It would take a while to completely unravel the manipulation that had taken place.

She, too, wondered about Natalie's true motives, and if the simple act of fooling everyone was her biggest gratification.

"So," Kate began, "now that you're no longer living in sin, have you thought about who's going to be Mommy, and who's Mama?"

Ellie nearly choked on her sip of wine.

Jordan patted her back lightly. "I didn't know this was a question you were worrying about."

"Come on, it's not such a far-fetched idea, is it? You were ready to adopt a teenager."

"That's right, a teenager who needed an emergency placement. And we would have done it, but this is different." She was aware of Ellie's gaze on her, thoughtful. "It requires some planning. And Ellie has had her new job for a few months only."

"But you're thinking about it, right?" Kate all but clapped her hands. Come to think of it, she'd probably had more to drink than Ellie. Aside from all that, she had a point as well. Pauline had brought up the subject one of the first times Ellie came to dinner. Since their plans to adopt Ariel hadn't worked out, there hadn't been a lot of time to reconsider, but Jordan had thought about it every once in a while, torn between a dream and sheer terror. It was mostly up to Ellie to make that decision, because her career was at such a critical stage.

"Not about what they're going to call us, not really," Ellie answered. Without hesitation, she added, "But maybe in a couple of years or so, it could happen."

"It could," Jordan agreed, relieved they were on the same page. They had just bought a house together, got married. They needed time to live in the present for a while—especially after this disturbing interlude.

All night, she had watched for signs of how Ellie was coping, which seemed okay. Later, when Ellie was asleep next to her, she allowed herself a glimpse into a future that might be. In a year or two.

⁂

The next morning, back at work, she achieved a tentative breakthrough. Jordan studied the computer screen with a sense of cautious excitement. She wasn't yet sure what it all meant, but it looked like her hunch was leading somewhere. She'd done some research on the buildings where Dinkins and Oswald, and the man they'd found guarding the hotel room, respectively, had lived.

It turned out both were owned by the same company, LHS, Leeden Housing Solutions. Leeden was part of an even bigger group that had invested billions in the past few years, buying buildings that fell in the category of affordable housing, as well as luxury suites, and a few hotels as well. It could be coincidence. The man Nina had shot had lived in a one-story house that his family owned, but there were other witnesses still waiting to testify.

She decided it was worth seeing Valerie Esposito again. The A.D.A. was frowning over a pile of files on her table, but she gestured for Jordan to sit down and offered her a coffee.

"Twice in as many days. To whom do I owe the pleasure?"

"I'm not sure yet, but I'd like to check the addresses of your witnesses again. Those who aren't in jail already, that is."

"Yeah. Thank God most of them are, but we don't want another one to end up dead. At least you saw the hotel room, and this was connected to Henderson's undercover gig anyway, so I don't think we'll lose any momentum here. If it becomes a trend, though, it could go all the way up to the boss."

"That's a federal case though."

"Yeah, but I still have to put some of these guys away, hopefully close to forever. What do you have?"

Jordan related the connection she had found regarding the apartments.

"It's thin at the moment, but there might be something there. I'll have Mindy print you a list."

"Thanks."

"How are things otherwise? Still in the honeymoon phase?"

"Yes, thank you very much. That's all you get on the subject."

Valerie laughed. "Yeah, that's what happens after marriage. You used to be fun."

Amused, Jordan thought about how much better her life was now that all the relationship drama, the questions and doubts, were firmly in the past.

"Like you'd know."

"I know enough," Valerie declared. "All right, let me know if that list leads to anything. Have a good day."

"You too."

She was about to get back to it, but the moment she stepped out of the elevator, so did April on the other side. She looked serious.

"Let's find Ellie and go somewhere we can talk in private?"

They went to an empty briefing room where April laid a folder on the table.

"First of all, this lady's set-up was extremely sophisticated. She made sure nothing would show up in a quick background check—address, DMV, social security number, all of those existed. But the real Natalie Morgan has been dead for almost a decade," she delivered the jaw-dropping news. Ellie was silent.

"What did she want?" Jordan asked.

"That, we haven't figured out yet. We have, however, found her car, abandoned by the highway. It was wiped clean."

"How could she do all this in such a short time? She must have had a partner. What about the neighbor? He seemed pretty taken with her."

"Yeah, but you talked to him as well. He might have a crush, but I don't think he knew about any of this."

"She lived with us for a couple of weeks. There are prints all over the house." Hers, and those of everyone at the party. Still, it should be possible to eliminate.

"Yeah, that would help," April agreed.

"She was cleaning all of the time. That will probably make it harder," Ellie remembered, her voice tinged with anger. "It's crazy. She was really into it, even leaving flowers on my parents' grave. She must have almost invested more money than she spent with the debit card. All those meals she cooked."

"She could have been stealing in other ways from you," April said. "Well, in a way she did. She lived rent-free with you, didn't pay anything for one of the apartments, and we are still trying to figure out where the payments for the second one came from. Perhaps she intended to stay longer, but then you spooked her."

"Now what?" Ellie sounded dejected.

"We are looking at other cases, similarities. She's too good to have done that for the first time. All the exposure, the set-up she needed to make this work...You don't start with a cop."

"Anything so far?" There was something chilling about what Natalie had done. Jordan didn't think she had murdered anyone, or was likely to do so—nevertheless, it took a sociopath to pull this off. She wasn't safe to be around. Certainly not for Ellie who had been forced to relive her grief all over again.

"One that sounded promising." It was unnerving to be on the other side of this equation, to be someone else's case. They'd both had their share of it already. "A woman found the daughter she had given up for adoption a long time ago. The daughter moved in, did all kinds of things for her, cooked, cleaned, ran errands...They even took a vacation together that the mom paid for. Then, all of a sudden, the daughter is gone. The cell phone number doesn't exist anymore. No one knew her at what was supposed to be her workplace, or the last known address before staying with Mom."

"Was there a letter?" Ellie asked.

"That's why she called the police. And it sounded very much like yours. She basically admits that it was a charade to begin with."

"I want to talk to that woman."

"I can set something up if you want."

"Yes, please do that. Thanks."

"Sure. I'll keep digging. This is certainly not a usual case. Normally it's pretty clear what the scam artist is after, and money is always on top of the list. All right, I'll get back to it."

Jordan and Ellie returned to their own desks, still absorbing what they'd just heard.

"What's in it for her?" Jordan asked.

"A sense of identity? I have no idea. That would be a case for Bethany."

Jordan gave her a quick sideways look just to make sure Ellie didn't mean she should contact Bethany in this. "I'm sure Dr. Burns could give us an expert opinion."

"Yeah. Probably."

"Are you going to be okay? There's something Derek and I have to check out."

"Yeah, of course." Ellie made a dismissive gesture. "I work here, too, remember?"

"I'm sorry. I didn't mean—"

"It's okay. I'll see you later."

Ellie had already turned her attention to a file on her desk, and Jordan was dismissed.

<hr />

"She'll be okay," Derek declared with more confidence than Jordan had at the moment. "This is not the worst you two have been through."

"No, but it's bad. She really thought they had a bond. Hell, I thought that."

"It sucks. You'll move on. Speaking of which, there's been a lot of baby talk lately…"

"Right. Kate was the one who brought it up."

"Oh, she's definitely not interested in that right now, going back to school and all. Things are good."

Jordan wondered about what might be between the lines of that statement, but she didn't prod, acknowledging that she and Ellie had enough on their plate at the moment.

"Ellie just made detective. Let's give it some time."

They were going to see William Leeden, the owner of LHS. Jordan's research hadn't brought up any connection to the men who died in two of their apartments, but she had found old news about a tax evasion scandal that led to a lot of firings and a complete reconstruction of the firm.

To her relief, Leeden didn't play coy and let them wait. He wasn't happy to see them either.

"We haven't had police in the house in a few years, and let me tell you, I'm relieved about that. I'm sure you're aware of what happened six years ago. A few of our accountants were happy to fill their own pockets, and it backfired badly on the firm. We made it back. That's all I can tell you."

"We're not here about that," Jordan told him. "You're aware of the deaths in two of your buildings?"

"I'm not sure what you mean. Those are a lot of apartments. Sadly, sometimes people die."

"These men were shot in the head while working for a sex trafficking ring out of said apartments. You do some sort of background check on prospective tenants?"

"That part of the building is in affordable housing. Sometimes it's people who need a second chance."

"Do the names Oswald and Dinkins ring a bell?"

He was silent for a few seconds. "I think I read about them—in the building on Newton?"

"That would be the one," Derek said. "Who would have taken care of those leases? And the one on Johnson Street?"

"I'm not sure I know by heart, but I can certainly find you that information."

"We'd appreciate that. You talked about second chances. So, you're aware if an applicant had, say, a record? Is there anywhere you'd draw the line?"

He shrugged. "You never know the whole story. We certainly don't deny housing to people who've made mistakes. As long as they served their time and have a job to pay the rent, I'm good."

Even if that job included selling human beings? Jordan wondered.

Marjorie Vaughn worked in an LHS office by the waterfront, and she confirmed that she did background checks on prospective tenants. She was in her fifties, shoulder-length hair, no make-up, and with a no-nonsense attitude about her.

"Middle-aged women are harmless and invisible to most people," she said with a shrug. "So they're comfortable, and tend to tell me things that they might not otherwise."

"Do you find they often lie on their applications?"

"All the time. But there's the Internet now, and of course public records...The past is hard to hide."

Jordan suppressed a sigh. She loved her present, having a life with the woman she loved and a job she was good at. None of it had deleted the fact that she came from a neglectful mother and a criminal father. Of course, they were talking about past issues on a different scale.

She had a brief thought for Natalie who had decided she didn't want any past at all, just one lie after the other.

"We're interested in particular former tenants of LHS."

"Yeah. Mr. Leeden warned me that it's about the dead men. I know that you usually need a warrant, but he told me to cooperate with you. We have nothing to hide."

"That's good to hear, Mrs. Vaughn."

"Ms.," she corrected Derek. "I'll pull up those records for you."

"Thank you. We appreciate it."

True to her word she was back a few minutes later with the printouts of the standard background checks for the names they had listed. People might tell Ms. Vaughn things, but they certainly left out some of them. Dinkins had not been forthcoming about his prior prison sentence in an assault case. On paper, the men looked fairly ordinary.

Dinkins and Oswald listed jobs in construction, and the man who had guarded the hotel room had given security guard as profession. In the notes, there was a mix of letters and numbers that looked like some sort of code.

"What does this mean?" Jordan showed the paper to Ms. Vaughn.

"Oh, just something for me. It's when Mr. Leeden meets with the applicant in person."

"He does that? Those are many apartments." He had said it himself.

"Yes. Sometimes. Let me see." She checked the note section for Dinkins' application. "And there's another one."

"Do you have any indication why Mr. Leeden would want to meet with these particular tenants?"

"I'm not sure. Sometimes it's about business. He's always trying to build and buy more, and someone with ties to construction might be helpful. Or perhaps they approached him—a security related job in exchange for reduced rent. Is there anything else I can do for you?"

"Could you find out who else Mr. Leeden met with in person? If you could email that to me..." Jordan handed her a card. "That's all for now, thank you Ms. Vaughn. We'll be in touch."

"Will we?" Derek asked when they were back in the car. "It's interesting for sure, but highly circumstantial. I'm not sure there's enough."

"You've been reading Kate's books? I have a feeling. Something is going to happen. And I think I might want to talk to Torres and have her ask Hank about Leeden. Meanwhile..." She stopped when her cell phone rang.

Chucky Mulveney wanted to talk.

Chapter
Seventeen

April had come through and given her the address. Joan Dempsey, the woman who had thought she'd finally found her daughter, agreed to meet Ellie.

She quickly went to see Maria Doss to explain the situation. To her relief, Maria didn't comment, just promised to call her if necessary.

Ellie went on her way, hoping to get closer to solving a mystery. Her drive took her about half an hour out of the city to a residential neighborhood. The door of the split-level house was opened to her the moment her finger was on the doorbell. Natalie's other likely victim was eager to talk.

"Ms. Dempsey, thank you for meeting me."

"It's no problem. I never imagined I'd hear anything about this ever again...let alone from someone who was fooled like I was."

Ellie wasn't sure she liked that interpretation, but she didn't have an alternative one. She followed Dempsey into an open concept living area, where the woman gestured for her to sit.

"I made coffee if you'd like one? This situation certainly calls for something stronger, but I suppose you're still on the clock."

"I'd love a coffee. Thank you." She was technically right, even though Natalie's case didn't have anything to do with Homicide. At least that's what they all thought.

Ms. Dempsey brought two steaming mugs to the coffee table where she'd already put milk and sugar. She sat down in an armchair across from Ellie.

"So, that woman has resurfaced again. Are you any closer to catching her?"

"We are following different leads at the moment." That was better, being the one in control, in charge. Not the naïve victim who had fallen for the sob story. But she had. Fallen. Ellie cleared her throat. "You said she left you a letter as well?"

"Oh yes. Can you imagine? What is wrong with people?" She handed Ellie a piece of paper that looked exactly like the one Natalie had left her. Reading the few lines, she recognized the style and some familiar content. *I wish I actually was your daughter.*

Did Natalie steal identities because she lacked a sense of her own?

"It was so bizarre," Dempsey remembered. "She knew that I had been trying to find my daughter, and what it meant to me. It was like she reveled in giving me that gift and then snatching it away again."

That was exactly Ellie's impression.

"Did she take money?"

"Some. She protested when I wanted to pay for the vacation, I insisted, she eventually accepted it. And she used one of my credit cards for a short time—without asking. She left with a necklace that was fairly expensive, but it never turned up in the pawn shops, or anywhere else, for that matter. Detective, can you tell me what this was really about?"

"I wish I could. My parents died in a car accident, years ago. Natalie, that's what she called herself, told me she was my sister, from a previous relationship my father had..." *God, I should have known.* "She had a picture. It's most likely been fabricated, like the rest of the story."

"I'm really sorry," Dempsey said, and, startled, Ellie realized there were tears in her eyes. Not now. It had become her mantra over the past few days. If she kept repeating it, the urge would go away. It had to.

"This time, you will find her, right?"

"Yes. We will."

There could be no doubt.

"You know, there is something else," Ms. Dempsey said. "I hadn't written a will before. I've been by myself for some time, and I didn't see the need, though when Liane came along, I thought about it. I talked about it with her, and like with the trip, she said no at first, but then agreed. I guess I'm lucky?"

Ellie wished there could have been something she knew for sure about Nathalie. Thalia. Liane. At least she knew this for sure—they wouldn't stop until they had all the answers.

"I'll let you know when we find her," she said.

❧

Jordan barely refrained from checking on Ellie once more. Marjorie Vaughn had come through and sent a list of names, prospective tenants Leeden had met with in person. Most of them were unfamiliar, but some stood out: Owens, Robertson's bodyguard, Oswald and the man who had been guarding the hotel room. Two of them were now dead. Someone had obviously tried to tie up lose ends.

If there was anything else Owens knew this fact might help them get to the bottom of it.

First, they met with Mulveney who nervously ushered them through the back entrance of *Rigley's*. They had once busted him for illegal gambling, and he had other entries on his rap sheet, but he'd been behaving for a few months—and how, he apparently had something to tell them.

"Please tell me we didn't come here for nothing," she said to him.

"Oh, you won't say this is nothing," Mulveney uttered. He had the appearance of someone who hadn't slept much in the past few days and was fighting the urge to look over his shoulder.

There was a wall behind him.

"First of all, I swear I had no idea all this bad shit was going on in this neighborhood."

"That's a surprise. We thought you know the neighborhood pretty well."

"I used to. We used to do our own thing here, but this…Those guys who were killed came from out of town, to do business for some big shot trafficker."

"I'm sorry, but that's not news to us," Jordan reminded him. "Focus?"

"The lease for *Rigley's* is up. I had some lawyer type come over and tell me not to renew it. I thought nothing about it, you know? When I took over earlier this year, the bar'd been here for over a decade, so I don't think I'm going anywhere, right? That's what I told him. Last night, they sent another guy. Told me I have twenty-four hours to vacate the premises." Mulveney lifted up his shirt.

Jordan saw Derek wince at the angry bruise that ran almost the length of his torso.

"Protect and serve, that's your job, right? I'd appreciate it right about now."

"Okay, we'll figure something out. Who are these people?"

"We rented from the family who owned the building at first, but they sold to one of those huge developers years ago."

"Would that be LHS?" Jordan asked. It would almost be too good to be true—if they could prove that LHS had been sheltering illegal activities under their roofs, they would go down. And this kind of business practices sounded much like taking care of loose ends.

"No, Cartwright Properties," he said to Jordan's disappointment. "I called them already and yelled—they deny having sent someone, but they still want me out. They're also going to raise the rent. So, what are you going to do about this mess?"

"They're going to come back to see if you upheld your end of the bargain. We'll be there. Don't worry."

"Never thought I'd hear that from a cop," Mulveney said. "I really want to believe you, but I'm not sure I do."

Jordan ignored the jibe. "Since we're already here, I'd like you to look at some pictures, see if you recognize anyone."

"Yeah, sure, glad to be of service."

Regardless of the sarcastic tone, he watched the slide show, stopping on Leeden.

"That's the big boss of Cartwright," he said. "I've never met him in person, but I know it's him."

"Thanks, Chucky. Now let's see how we can properly welcome them."

⟨⟩

Ellie was grateful for a busy day that involved more research on Cartwright Properties and, eventually, a meeting with A.D.A. Esposito.

The company had started out as a family business twenty years ago but had been bought out by its competitor LHS seven years ago. In the meantime, LHS had acquired more and more property in the area, including the buildings on Johnson Street and Newton, and the one that housed *Rigley's*. Areas with higher crime rates seemed to be their specialty—in the time they owned the buildings, rent had gone up, though it didn't seem like they had done much in terms of renovations. The crime statistics had changed slightly in accordance with the general trend, but it seemed like they were overcharging. The people who could pay were those who made money on the side—like Mulveney, or Oswald and Dinkins.

Another couple of searches turned up the fact that Owens had rented an apartment not far from *Rigley's*, in addition to the living space his job as Robertson's bodyguard had bought him. Lastly, Cartwright also owned a building housing several businesses, including a hairdresser, a Laundromat, and a pub.

She also looked deeper into the LHS scandal and put everything together to hopefully convince Esposito that they needed to take a hard look at the company's finances.

Before she went to see her, Ellie took a moment to reflect on her conversation with Ms. Dempsey. She couldn't help wondering how many more there were, who had opened their doors to Natalie. How many more it would take for her to stop, and what would be the catalyst to make her. Ellie shook her head. It didn't matter. They'd find her first, and she'd have a lot to answer for.

⌒

After they had set up everything to welcome the goons Leeden had sent, Jordan went back to the department where she inadvertently crashed Ellie's meeting with A.D.A. Esposito.

Whatever challenges they had to face together and individually, she couldn't help the moment of pride at seeing proof that Ellie was well coming into her own in the job she'd always wanted. Ellie, of course, had many other things on her mind today, but Valerie saw through her. Perhaps it wasn't all that hard, because she wore her heart on her sleeve when it came to Ellie.

"Detective Carpenter, did you need anything, or did you just come here to watch us?"

Ellie didn't say anything, but she seemed a bit flustered.

"A good day to you too, Counselor. Where are we on those warrants?"

"Still a bit thin what you have, but I see where you're going with this. It's coming together."

"Good. These people bought up properties all over town. There's no way they had no clue what was going on in any of them."

"There are too many dead bodies for it to be a coincidence," Ellie agreed. "Owens' name came up again, too."

"Interesting." Jordan picked up one of the sheets Ellie had brought, a list of buildings owned by LHS/Cartwright. Outside the ones she already knew, another caught her eye, the place where Kim Geller, also a tenant on Newton where Dinkins and Oswald had been killed, worked as a hairdresser. She had led them to *Rigley's* and Mulveney in another case. "Definitely too many connections. Keep digging—and we'll see what the folks who roughed up Mulveney will tell us..." She checked her watch. "Well, later tonight."

"You need me for that?"

"No, you keep doing what you're doing." She wanted to ask how Ellie's encounter with Natalie's other victim had gone, but not in front of Valerie. Since that case was of a highly private nature, she was going to wait until they were home—which could be a while. "Thanks. I'll let you get back to it."

"Could have done that on the phone."

Valerie clearly meant for her to hear those words. Jordan didn't think she needed to comment on them.

She would go home to shower and change and then come back to meet Derek at *Rigley's*. When she was ready to leave, Ellie still sat at her desk with piles of printouts and files.

"You'll be okay?" she asked.

"Yes. It's moving along. I'll let you know if we find something."

"All right then. I'll see you sometime later tonight—or in the morning, depending on how it goes."

"Yeah. Be careful."

"Always am."

Given that they were almost alone, Jordan dared a quick kiss and reluctantly turned to leave.

"Come here for a second?" Ellie asked, resigned. When Jordan perched on the edge of her desk, she sighed. "This," she said, indicating the papers, "is good for me. It keeps me from thinking about this whole mess every moment of the day. I'll be okay, but right now I'm not sure I am. I am so pissed. How could this happen to me? How could I let her trick me?"

"She's a pro," Jordan reminded her. "It appears that she has done this many times, and people like that...They find a weakness and zoom in on it."

"Yeah. I hate that I was such an easy target."

"Everyone believed her. And if it makes you feel better—that's how Darby worked, and he got away with it for too long." Even dead, the man was a shadow never too far behind. He had been too eager offering solutions when Jordan's life was a mess. Natalie had figured out what Ellie wished for, and she had a good story ready.

"No, that doesn't make me feel better. You think she might have killed anyone?"

"I don't know. It's hard to tell at this point."

"Right. You have to go."

"Yes. Hang in there. We'll talk later."

Chapter Eighteen

Driving to *Rigley's* forty-five minutes later, Jordan acknowledged she was deeply unsettled by all those loose ends—some unconnected, but they all bothered her. Natalie, or whatever her real name was. They needed to find her before she could mess with someone else's life, or, worse, put some sort of bigger plan in motion. She had been in their home. Perhaps she shouldn't have linked her to Darby—she was freaking herself out.

While they might be getting closer to finding out who had killed Dinkins, Oswald, and the man on Johnson Street, Isabel Combs remained missing. Nina Torres had been right, she thought. That was what mattered, to give closure to the families, bring down the perpetrators. But in this case, the ones who killed the traffickers could be just as bad. They couldn't stand back and pretend these murders had never happened.

Officers Casey Lyons and Wes Martin were guarding *Rigley's* at this moment. It was early for the goons to show up, the twenty-four hours not up yet—but maybe they would return earlier if they found that Mulveney made no effort to move. It might be that the episode with Natalie had made her paranoid, but she had a bad feeling, the setup reminiscent of the situation at the safehouse in which Kate's fiancé Jensen Baker had been killed. An ambush orchestrated by a man who was now serving a life sentence, her own biological father.

It was ironic that Ellie had been vulnerable because she wished to have family by blood in her life.

It was the complete opposite for Jordan—hers made everything infinitely more complicated.

When the email from April appeared in her inbox, Ellie wasn't sure if she should be excited or upset. No matter how much leeway Jordan, or anyone else for that matter, was willing to give her, she felt like she had failed. Her parents, Madeline, her mother's friend who had doubted Natalie from the start, and herself. She hadn't even known how much she'd wanted that connection, something Natalie had tapped into and exploited to her advantage—but what advantage, really? A bit of money spent and the satisfaction of fooling the people around her? What was the endgame?

She opened the mail to find a couple of photos attached.

I doubt that this is her mother, April wrote. *That lady is a picture from a stock photo site. Very well made though.*

Just more proof at how she'd failed to pay attention. Natalie had created her persona well enough to pass a basic background check, but she had left traces. Ellie wrote a quick *thank you* and then surveyed the files still on her desk. She could return to them tomorrow...but the house would be empty for at least a few more hours. Ellie went to get herself a coffee from the break room and went back to work.

"So, Kate and I were talking..." Derek began. They had settled in, ready to spend the next few hours waiting.

"Talking is good."

"Yeah. We were thinking about a weekend in Vegas and wondering if you and Ellie wanted to join us."

Inside *Rigley's*, Mulveney had closed for the evening. They were watching the back, another pair of detectives at the front entrance. Jordan nearly dropped her paper cup with the coffee in it.

"Say that again. No, wait. Now?"

"Why not? It's been a pretty rough case. As for Ellie's pretend sister, there is no news. I'm sure you guys could use some time away. Just a weekend."

"A weekend is enough time to get into trouble," Jordan mused. "Do I sense ulterior motives?" She was intrigued, and a bit alarmed at the same time. Kate and Derek had broken up and then got back together not long ago. She wondered whose idea this trip was. Kate, after all, had revealed that she would prefer to keep things casual.

"The motive is to play a little blackjack and have some drinks in a bar where it's unlikely we run into a supervisor. Come on. It'll be fun."

This looked more and more like a cover story. Jordan could count the occasions when she'd seen Carroll at the *Code 7* or the *Night Shift*, on one hand.

"You bought a ring. Are you sure this is the right—"

"Carpenter, you don't know everything. There is no ring."

"If you say so." Jordan had received the message that this was not a subject to continue. "All right, sure, it would be fun, though I'm not entirely sure about the timing. I think Ellie is going to need some time to absorb everything that happened."

"She can take all the time she needs. Friday to Sunday. That's all."

"I'll talk to her."

"Thanks. That's all I wanted."

Jordan wasn't convinced he had told her the whole truth, and she wasn't sure they would want to get in the middle of a rejected proposal, but now wasn't the time.

A black van passed them by and came to a halt in one of the parking spaces behind *Rigley's*.

"Showtime," she said, which might have been an unfortunate metaphor.

Vegas? She'd settle for a quick, clean bust, and some quality time with Ellie later. No more complications.

⁂

Ellie jumped when the phone on Jordan's desk rang. Seeing that she was closest to it, she got up and answered.

"This is Detective Harding."

"Hello," the woman said reluctantly. "I got this number from Detective Carpenter."

"She's not here right now. Can I give her a message...or can I help you?"

"Maybe...she said to call if anything came up. I'm not sure."

"What's your name?"

"Kim Geller. I work at the hairdresser on the corner of Newton and Bradford."

"Ms. Geller, what can I do for you?" The name was familiar to Ellie. Geller lived in the same building where Dinkins and Oswald had been found dead, and the hair salon was situated in another building owned by Cartwright/LHS.

"I'm not sure, but I was about to close, and this black van has been circling the block four times now. You know about the murders in the neighborhood. I'm scared."

With the operation going down at *Rigley's*, possibly at this moment, and the other recent crimes, she probably had reason to be. Her landlord was likely implicated, both privately and with the business.

"Why don't you lock up and I come by and take a look around? I can give you a ride home."

"That would be great, thank you so much."

"Did you get a license plate?"

"Yes, I wrote it down."

Ellie did the same, intent on having it checked right away.

"All right. Please stay away from the windows. I'll be there in about fifteen minutes—but if you feel threatened, call 911 first."

"I'll do that. Thanks, Detective."

"You're welcome."

⁂

There was only a lone bicyclist on the street when Ellie arrived at the hair salon. The backup unit she had asked for was on its way. After parking her car, she headed across the street to the front door with the "closed" sign in the window and rang the bell. Kim Geller opened right away and locked behind them.

"Thank God you're here. I didn't know what to do."

"That's okay, Ms. Geller, we'll figure it all out."

They were standing to the side of the huge window, as Ellie had instructed Geller earlier. "Does the name Leeden Housing Solutions ring a bell?"

"Yes, of course, they own this building, and the one I live in. Are you saying—"

Out of the corner of her eye, Ellie saw the black van, slowing down as it neared the shop.

"Get down!"

She pushed Kim Geller behind the counter and to the floor the moment the shots rang out and pulverized the window. Seeing that the woman was curled up underneath the counter, she took out her gun and inched closer to the front door, but the van was gone. Holstering her weapon, Ellie took a deep breath, before she went back to check on Geller and wait for backup to arrive. This could have gone many different ways.

Chucky Mulveney looked on, somewhat in awe, when police officers led the two men who had come to collect out of *Rigley's* in handcuffs. The situation had been resolved without a single gunshot, a success in Jordan's book. If those men were willing to turn on their boss, they might have all the information they needed to close two cases.

She patted Mulveney's shoulder.

"See what happens when you act like a law-abiding citizen?"

He snorted.

"Yeah. Mostly," she amended. "I bet the profits went up since you got all your licenses in order."

"That was freaky," Mulveney admitted. "In many ways."

"Well, you're still here, and so is your business. You're welcome."

"Right. Thank you, Detective. Just make sure they don't come back again."

Their banter was interrupted when the disturbing information came over the scanner: Shots fired at Newton and Bradford—Kim Geller's workplace.

Chapter
Nineteen

When they arrived with blazing sirens, the hairdresser's front window had been shot out, a million shards all over the sidewalk. What Jordan hadn't expected was Ellie to emerge from the back room, and her reaction reflected her surprise more than she would have liked.

"What the hell...what are you doing here?"

"Um...work? What I had in mind was a quiet evening with paperwork, but then Ms. Geller called your phone. I was going to give her a ride home, but it never came to that." Before Jordan could comment, Ellie continued, "I ran the car, and they seem related to LHS. A BOLO is going out as we speak. They're not getting out of the city. When Ms. Geller called, they were just circling the block. Unfortunately, shortly after I arrived, they were trying to shoot their way in. Relax. I'm fine. So is she."

"I wasn't going to say anything," Jordan defended herself which got her a raised eyebrow from Derek.

"Good. I guess this means more paperwork..."

The vehicle of the men who had destroyed the store window was stopped minutes later. Of the arrests made that night, one of them was willing to talk, and his story shone a new, disturbing light on the murders, and LHS's business practices as a whole.

Ellie watched the interrogation from behind the window, thrilled at how the information she had gathered, backed up tonight's operation. Aside from the legit hair salon, Kim Geller's landlord owned a side business that involved escort services and prostitution.

It was late, everyone was tired, but she admired the way Jordan got the man to reveal these many details.

LHS had found a lucrative business in renting out to individuals and businesses that they were able to blackmail—once the authorities got too close, they diverted attention. For sure, there were many ways that misfortune could come to players like Oswald and Dinkins. Their murderers didn't have the wellbeing of the women they harmed in mind—just their own. Hardly anything was what it seemed at first sight...and with that, her brief reprieve from her own situation was over.

She knew this episode wouldn't change any of her plans in the long run—continue on her career path, start a family with Jordan once they were both ready, enjoy the life they were building together. She had so much to be grateful for. Why couldn't she act like it?

The next morning would bring more arrests and paperwork, but eventually, they were able to go home.

Ellie stood by the kitchen island, pouring a glass of water for both of them, when the email came in.

Holy Shit. April wasn't holding back. *We widened the search, and there are more than a dozen cases that sound eerily familiar. Meet me tomorrow?*

Ellie tossed the phone aside and started to cry, fairly embarrassed about it, but unable to stop. Jordan silently embraced her, which felt good, but didn't make her stop either. Perhaps she could chalk up part of her reaction to the stress of getting shot at. Ellie wasn't kidding herself. It had been stressful without a doubt, but her tears came from another source, something that had been building up over the past few days.

It had been the perfect story—in which Patrick Harding had done nothing wrong. After all he didn't know about the pregnancy, and if he had, he would have done all the right things. What counted in the present was that Ellie had a biological sister, family that connected her to her parents more than their best friends, Madeline, and her family—or so Ellie had foolishly believed.

She felt bad for even putting so much emphasis on this detail when it was her chosen family that had been there for her through the worst, and the best times. She'd let them down. There was still the deep sadness about having something taken away from her when she hadn't even known how much she had longed for it—and the anger that was still trying to work its way through.

"I'm sorry," she finally managed. "This is pathetic."

"Not really. When you throw a glass against the wall, then we can talk about pathetic." There was a smile in Jordan's voice, and also a reminder that so far, they had taken on any challenge coming their way. "You have the right to be angry, and sad. But she messed with the wrong people. We'll get her."

"Yeah." Ellie reached for the roll of paper towels and tore off one to wash her face.

"I think I've had enough of this day. Meet me in bed?"

"I look forward to it."

Later, Jordan told her about the suggestion Derek had made. Ellie could see the wisdom in getting out of town for a weekend, though she was wondering about something.

"He's going to ask her to marry him, right? And we both know that could go either way."

"He denies it, but I'm not so sure. In any case...I think we should go. April knows her job, and otherwise there's not much we can do for now."

"Yeah." Ellie sighed. "I can't help thinking she's not done."

"It doesn't matter. We'll put an end to it either way. I'm sure she's moving on to the next target," Jordan mused. "I guess that is something we need to realize. She doesn't care...at all."

"True. Creepy." Ellie snuggled closer. "I guess we'll go to Vegas then."

"After another mountain of paperwork, that is."

By noon, William Leeden was in custody, and two more of his hired minions had given a full confession. They had purchased the gun used to kill Dinkins and Oswald on the black market. How it had gotten from the evidence locker into the seller's hands, they had no idea.

Lieutenant Carroll called a meeting with all investigators involved to discuss a strategy going forward with what they had learned.

After twenty minutes, a knock on the door preceded Officer Marshall into the room.

"I'm sorry. Jordan, there's someone here for you," she said. "Says it can't wait."

Jordan pushed back her chair as quietly as possible and left, wondering if April had a lead. They had made plans to meet her in the afternoon. To her surprise, the woman sitting in the visitor's chair wasn't her. Jordan could hardly believe her eyes.

"Ms. Combs?"

"I asked to speak to the lead investigator, the one who put Hank away."

"I'm Detective Carpenter. We've been looking for you. Your mother—"

Isabel's eyes filled with tears. "They said no one would come for us, ever, and if anyone tried, that they'd kill them. I had to make sure. I had to know it's over."

"It is," Jordan told her. "I think we should call your mom, have you checked out, and then...I guess you understand we have some questions." She waved over Libby Marshall, who was about to leave, and asked her to drive Isabel to the hospital. There were no obvious injuries, but with what she knew about the case, she wasn't going to take any chances.

Isabel didn't object to anything she said.

"Please, tell me, where have you been?"

"I was lucky," Isabel said. "When I got out, I didn't know where to go. I was terrified that they'd find me or come after my family. I spent some time in a shelter, and I met someone there who got me to a place that was safe for a while. I didn't know what to do...until I walked past a store, and there was a TV on. It said you solved the case."

There were still holes in that story, but they could certainly wait.

"Did you see who killed the two men in the apartment, Oswald and Dinkins?" Jordan asked.

"Yes. I'll never forget their faces."

Once she had seen her mother and a doctor, a line-up would be a good idea.

"Okay. I'll notify your mom, and I'll join you at the hospital. I'm glad you came here."

Isabel gave her a smile, though the sadness in her expression was heartbreaking. She had made it through the worst, but it would be a long time before anything would be close to normal in her life.

"You are so much stronger than them," she said, considering it a success that Isabel didn't disagree.

❧

Nina Torres called to congratulate her on closing the case, and a few hours later, so did Bethany.

"Well, there were a lot of details that had to come together. Including Isabel Combs walking right up to my desk."

"How is she?" Bethany asked.

"Physically—she'll be okay. The rest, it's the same nightmarish stuff as with the others. At least she has her mom."

"Yeah. That way, she's better off than most of them."

Jordan realized that she might be aware of Nina's background. It wasn't up to either of them to bring it up in this context. In any case, it was good to know that some of these stories had a chance at a better ending.

"True."

After they ended the conversation, it was almost time to meet April. They hadn't had time to read all of her dossier yet, but from what Jordan had seen, there was a clear pattern to Natalie's behavior. She seemed to revel in other people buying her story and persona more than anything. Sometimes she had sought a romantic relationship with her subject, sometimes pretended to be long lost family, always inserted herself deeply into her targets' lives. The amounts of money she had gotten out of them were relative, though enough to trigger a fraud investigation.

If April was right, she had done her spiel for almost a decade. What did that mean for them?

April came by shortly before five, and they retreated to the break room.

"I went over all of these with a fine-toothed comb," she said. "The silver lining is that we can now tie them together."

"You have any leads as to where she is?" Jordan asked. Ellie looked pensive.

"She has fallen off the face of the Earth as it seems." April sighed. "She alters her appearance completely, steals identities. By the time people realize something's up, she's usually gone. No offense. She's good. I've never seen anything like it. Since she's not going after money specifically, that makes it even harder to trace. I just wanted you to know we're not letting up."

"We appreciate that," Ellie said. "So, there are all those cases, but we have no idea where she is now."

"I'm afraid so. I'm really sorry."

"She makes clean cuts, right? Finishes one job, and then it's off to something else completely."

"I'm not sure she'd call it a job," April said. "It seems to me that to her, it's more of a lifestyle."

Ellie shook her head. "I think I'd be fine if I never saw that woman again, but...she did this with so many people. I want her to pay."

Jordan could only agree.

Chapter Twenty

Once the flights were booked, and bags packed for a weekend stay, Ellie actually managed to get excited. She was looking forward to spending time with Kate, whom she didn't see often since she had left the force to study law.

That, and she could use all the distraction, from the Natalie issue and from the recent cases.

Perhaps after that, they could revisit an idea that would require a lot of planning, financially and otherwise, should they go through with it. A year or two. It didn't seem all that long. They would always be busy, and their respective approach to family would be the same as well.

It would be important not to miss the right moment. There was always a right moment for everything.

They had agreed to meet Kate and Derek later for dinner after checking in—enough time to shower, relax, and make otherwise use of the king-size bed.

Jordan was half-dressed, Ellie still in her robe when a knock on the door propelled them into action. She quickly tied the belt while Jordan, still barefoot, but wearing pants and a shirt, went to answer.

Kate walked into the room with a huge smile and a bottle of champagne.

"I know we said we were going to meet up later, but we kind of need you now. Come on, Ellie, get dressed already. It's happening now..."

She held up her hand to showcase the ring.

"I was right!" Jordan said. "Tell him I knew all along. We'll be right there."

At least something was leading to a somewhat unexpected, happy ending.

⁂

"I'm really sorry I lied to you." They were less than ten minutes away from the big moment, and apparently, Derek needed to get this off his chest.

"No problem. You knew I didn't believe you, right?"

"Of course. You're scary good that way."

Jordan laughed. "It's only scary for people who lie, but I understand you wanted to keep this between you and Kate for as long as possible. I'm happy for you. You deserve it. There's something that's bothering me though."

"What's that?"

She stepped forward and straightened his tie. "There. Now you're ready."

"Thank you for being here."

"I wouldn't want to miss this for anything. Now go say yes, so we can properly celebrate."

They ended their conversation with a quick hug between two people who usually weren't too comfortable with the gesture—but it seemed fitting.

⁂

After the papers were signed, they retreated to the hotel for more champagne and a bit of gambling. Jordan joined Derek at a blackjack table while Kate and Ellie tried out several machines, so far, with acceptable losses.

"How are you doing?" Kate asked, out of the blue. She seemed self-conscious about the question a moment later. "I feel like I should give you some context. This—it's the best day of my life, something that, after Jensen...I didn't think could still happen for me. You're my best friend. I want you to be just as happy."

"I am. I promise."

Kate took a sip of her cocktail before she hit the button again to start the wheels spinning. This time, seven dollars were added to their win. Surprisingly, another twenty after that.

"There will always be those fuckers that thrive on other people's pain. The important thing is that we don't let them win."

Ellie was well aware that Kate's words encompassed more than Natalie's con. She agreed wholeheartedly.

"Never. So, let's do some more winning."

It turned out their philosophy didn't work so well on the machine. However, Derek and Jordan joined them a moment later, and he was waving a check with a triumphant smile.

"Keep this one," he told Ellie with a nod to Jordan. "She's good luck."

"I didn't do anything."

"Yeah, I know. And modest, too." Ellie knew she had plenty of reasons to feel lucky and grateful. She almost wasn't jealous over the numbers on that check.

"More champagne for all," Derek declared, and no one disagreed.

Perhaps this was what Natalie hoped to achieve someday but had never managed: Finding a circle of people who loved her for who she was.

Ellie couldn't bring herself to feel sorry for her, but the realization went a long way to ease her own pain.

It had taken Ellie a while not to think of the relative calm of the next few days as the calm before just another storm. She was happy for Kate and Derek who seemed to have taken the right turn for good, even with all the challenges they faced. Work was never slow. She had exactly the life she had chosen. No one could take that away from her.

They had met at the *Night Shift* again, where Jordan revealed that Jack was almost ready to open the re-built *Code 7* under a different name.

"I'm so glad he gave up on calling it Carpenter's." She laughed. "I would have never lived that one down."

"If we go by cases closed, he should have called it Carpenter & Henderson at least," Derek deadpanned. "No one's going to come close to the record in the next few years."

"Oh, I don't know." Casey Lyons pulled herself a chair and sat at the table. "Harding seems to be well on her way."

"No offense, but that's not even close."

"We'll talk again in a couple of years. She always gets what she wants," Casey declared. "In any case," she directed at Jordan, "Your dad's doing a great job. It will be good to go back there...and for the neighborhood."

"Yeah. I think so too."

"So, what else is on the horizon?"

"I don't know," Ellie said. "There's not a lot going on at the moment, and that's a relief, after everything. Two years from now...many things could happen." She caught Jordan's smile on her. The number had almost become code, and here, with her closest friends, she felt safe enough to say it out loud. "We might even have a child."

"Yeah, you just got married, take your time with that," Casey advised. "You know what's going to happen. No more sex."

She earned some laughter. Ellie thought that was fairly unimaginable. The smile still on her face, she reached for her phone when it buzzed in her purse. The caller ID, however, put a frown on her face. She appreciated April keeping them up to date about the investigation, but frankly, she didn't need to know every little detail as long as there was no solid lead on Natalie.

"Excuse me. Hi." She had caught April before her call went to voicemail. "What's up?"

"Looks like our girl is still in the county. Face recognition software is a magical thing."

"Where is she?" Ellie asked, and all of a sudden, everyone at the table went silent.

"We don't know exactly, but we're close."

"That's good news."

"It is. You want to meet us? I'll text you an address. We're about to set up something."

"Sure, I'll see you in a bit."

When she hung up, everyone's expectant gazes were on her.

"That was April," she said. "They have a lead."

Chapter
Twenty-One

Natalie hummed to herself as she drove along the scenic route early that morning, nothing to distract her from the beautiful landscape. She loved driving. It cleared her mind, from the latest persona, the latest connections she was about to leave behind. It worked every time. Her peace of mind was disturbed by the sudden appearance of a police car. She sat straighter in her seat, still expecting the vehicle to pass her by.

It didn't.

When the lights indicated for her to stop, Natalie let out a curse, but she pulled up on the side of the road, keeping a cordial smile in place. She had nothing to be worried about. If the cop ran a quick check, they wouldn't find anything out of the ordinary. Natalie always made sure of that, and, well, it had worked the other time. She'd known that either Jordan or Ellie would try to be on the safe side, not that it had helped them.

She rolled down the window, realizing the young man seemed barely out of the academy. Natalie relaxed. This should be easy.

"Good morning, Officer," she said. "What can I do for you?"

"License and registration, please."

"Of course. Can I ask what this is about? I'm pretty sure I wasn't too fast."

Stop, she told herself. She knew better than to argue with the officer, even if he looked no older than twenty.

He studied her papers and then looked back at her. "Ms. Nadine Sawyer?"

"Yes. Is there a problem?"

"Please wait. I'll be right back."

Natalie tapped her fingers on the steering wheel, resisting the impulse to cut her losses and run. She knew those papers were perfect. It would be stupid to hit the gas pedal and draw any more attention to herself.

After a few minutes that felt like an hour, the young officer returned.

"Ms. Sawyer? Please step out of the car. I need you to come with me to the station."

"Wow, that sounds serious. Can't you just write me a ticket? I'm in a bit of a hurry."

"Step out of the car, now," he repeated.

Natalie saw that his hand went to his gun. Easy, she told herself. This will all go away. After all, she'd lived with cops for weeks, and they didn't suspect her. She'd gotten herself out of worse messes.

"Okay. I'm sure we'll clear this all up in a heartbeat."

"There are several outstanding traffic violations in your name, Ms. Sawyer. I'm sorry, but I need you to come with me."

Natalie felt her jaw drop. Acting demure for the time being, she mentally slapped herself. How was that even possible? Nadine Sawyer was a goody two shoes—no way had she not paid her parking tickets. From what Natalie knew, Nadine wouldn't even let herself get a parking ticket.

Yet, she was in the back of a police car.

This wasn't good.

It wasn't good, but Natalie was determined to make the best of her situation. They'd have to tell her what the damage was, and she'd pay them cash, at the worst. As long as she could stay Nadine, things were good. The cops at the small station were polite. This was routine—her fault that she hadn't researched Nadine enough. This couldn't happen again.

She had to get herself out of here before they took finger-prints.

Natalie was lucky to look the part of an allegedly harmless woman in her late thirties to early forties—they had brought her to an interview room instead of a holding cell. She assumed that in a small place like this, they'd handle things differently. After about ten minutes, a woman in civilian clothes joined her. She wore her curly blonde hair in a pony-tail, jeans and a white shirt.

"Good morning, Ms. Sawyer," she said.

Natalie smiled. The other woman's expression remained serious.

"Good morning. Frankly, I still don't understand why I'm here. Your officer said there were some tickets? Can't I just pay them and leave? You're not mistaking me for an escaped felon, are you?"

Now, the woman smiled back at her.

"You tell me, Natalie. Oh, by the way, I'm Detective Cassidy. I'll be right back with you, but first, there's someone who'd like to have a word with you."

"That's not my name! It's Nadine!" Natalie called after her.

"Yeah, whatever you say."

"You have no right to hold me!"

At the door, Detective Cassidy turned.

"Let's see, there's identity theft and fraud to start with. Don't worry, I have lots of good reasons...and messing with friends of mine did not help."

Ellie stepped into the room and closed the door behind herself. They had been up all night, finding Natalie and setting the trap for her. She had expected a myriad of emotions for the moment she'd see Natalie again...but Natalie, the illusion she'd presented, was gone. The woman sitting in that chair, giving her that arrogant smile even though her foot was tapping the floor lightly, wasn't her sister. She was a stranger, a criminal.

Ellie was done mourning what had never been.

"I assume you want the long story from me," Natalie said. "How I found you."

"I already know what. You like to use newspaper articles for your research."

"Why you?"

Ellie shrugged. "I'm sorry, but you're overestimating yourself. We found the other victims. I have the answers I need. I don't think you have anything to add."

"Oh, but you don't know that. Aren't you curious? I could have chosen to be a long lost relative from Jordan's messed up family...of course they aren't dead, but they never gave a damn either, so—"

"Shut up," Ellie told her, fairly proud she'd made Natalie flinch without even raising her voice. "Leave Jordan out of this. None of this is a surprise. Of course you'd go the easier route, and you know why? You aren't that good after all."

"Oh no? I lived in your house. I cooked you dinner. I fooled you."

"For a while, yes."

Natalie looked pleased with herself.

"You want to know why I came all the way here?"

"I don't know, to take another look at your almost sister? To imagine what could have been, little orphan Ellie no longer alone?"

"See, that's what you got wrong. I was never alone. For a moment, I might have thought I needed you, but I never did." Ellie looked up to hold the gaze of the woman who had inserted herself into her life, a fake. "You're done, Natalie. I wanted to be the one to tell you—for myself, and for all the others. Have a nice day."

She walked out of the room while Natalie sat in stunned silence.

⁜

"Great job," April said. "Now that the fun part is over, our local colleagues and I will have to deal with this egomaniac all day. What about you? You're a long way from home."

Jordan looked over to Ellie who stood leaning against the wall, looking calm, but tired.

"Yeah, I think we'll stay for the night and head home tomorrow after breakfast. Why don't you come join us at the hotel when you're done here? We could have dinner."

"Sounds great," April confirmed. "See you guys later."

They walked out of the building and down the concrete steps into the sunlight.

"Now that it's over for real, how are you feeling?" Jordan asked.

"Lucky," Ellie said and pulled her close for a kiss.

Chapter
Twenty-Two

April came by later for a quick update, but having an early start the next day, she didn't stay for dinner after all. Jordan and Ellie decided on a quiet evening with room service, taking their meal out on the small balcony of their room.

Ellie's mind was still reeling from the events of the past forty-eight hours. Did she have all the answers she wanted? Maybe not, but Natalie wouldn't be able to pull her scheme on other unsuspecting people in the future. The rest was for April's team to figure out.

"I think there's someone I should call," she said. "They'll notify her anyway, but I feel like I should talk to her."

Jordan seemed to sense that she needed to get it out of the way right now. She nodded, so Ellie picked up her phone and pulled up a number she'd found only recently, of a woman she shared a rather unique experience with.

The phone was answered after a couple of rings.

"Mrs. Dempsey, this is Detective Harding. I'm sorry to call you this late, but there's something I wanted to tell you."

"Honestly, I didn't expect to hear from you again...does that mean...?"

"We arrested her today. The detective on the case will contact you, but I wanted you to know as soon as possible...We got her, and she'll go to prison for what she did."

"That's good news, then. Thank you so much, Detective. Did she say...why?"

"My colleagues are still interrogating her, but I assume they'll bring in a psychiatrist as well. It seems like people believing her stories was the gratification she wanted. Whenever someone was asked too many questions, she moved on."

"I guess that's all we'll ever know."

Mrs. Dempsey sounded wistful. Ellie could easily understand why: She hadn't been able to solve a question that had been fundamental in her life.

"Would you like to find your daughter?" That was perhaps a strange question to ask, but Ellie was in a strange mood today.

"For a long time, I thought it would be better for her if I just let her be, let her live her life however she chose...and that I didn't have the right."

Yes, Natalie had a knack for zooming in on these kinds of insecurities.

"And now?"

"Is there any way you can help me?"

"I can ask around, check with a few friends. I'm sorry I can't promise you anything."

"I understand that. Thank you."

"It's no problem. I'll email you if we find anything. Have a good night."

"You too, Detective."

Ellie looked up to find Jordan studying her, and she waited. For gentle criticism, maybe, because Jordan knew better than anyone else that dealing with one's biological parents wasn't always easy. This was different, though. Mrs. Dempsey had made a decision very early in her daughter's life, and unlike Kathryn, she hadn't exposed her child to neglect.

Or maybe it wasn't about that at all. They sure had been given a lot to think about, family, and what it meant to either of them. What it would mean for both of them, someday, in a year or two.

She sat back down and picked up her glass and took a sip.

"Something's on your mind."

Jordan hesitated. "There has to be a lot on *your* mind right now."

"Most of it was sorted out the moment I walked into that room and saw her. There were no surprises after that—but I wasn't kidding when I said I know who my real family is. You are."

"What if we don't wait two years, or even one?"

The question Jordan blurted out made so much sense to Ellie, it occurred to her that it had been on her mind as well, in the background, sometimes at the forefront. She felt calm about it, perhaps because for them, it was a logical next step.

"That was never set in stone anyway. We could start by getting some information."

"You're serious?"

"Yes, of course. I was serious when we tried to adopt Ariel...and I am now. I know a lot of people say it's a bad world to bring a child into, but I still believe we can make a difference. We can raise a child that will be an adult who makes a difference."

"We talked about this before, a little. We never talked about who's going to have the baby."

Ellie hadn't missed the sudden anxious tone of Jordan's voice. She thought she knew what it meant, and what she needed to say.

"Talk to me."

"It might be the case. It's more than that because there will always be a case. And your career is just taking off, this is why we said we'd wait in the first place, but for me, it might be the last chance."

"I understand. Let's do it."

Jordan was on her feet the next moment, pulling Ellie up and into her arms.

"I thought this would be more complicated," she confessed.

"Hey. When have I ever been complicated?"

Jordan laughed. "You're right." As they sat back down, holding on to each other's hands, she continued, "It might get a little complicated though. With the job and Kathryn both."

"But that doesn't change two years from now, does it? I'm sure Casey can give us some tips once we're there. Everything else, we'll figure out. I promise you."

"I believe you."

Perhaps this had been the answer she'd hoped for, and it had nothing to do with this case and Natalie's motivations—and everything with the future that lay ahead for Ellie and Jordan.

It was looking bright.

About the Author

B arbara Winkes writes sapphic crime drama and Christmas romance. She loves writing characters who get the job done, whether it's stopping a predator or saving cherished traditions—while still making time for love. She lives with her wife in Quebec City.

barbarawinkes.com

Also by Barbara Winkes

The Crossing Lines Trilogy
Undercover
Redemption
Vengeance

The Connected Series
Promised to the Queen
Drawn to the Enemy
Tempted by the Protector

Kelli & Merin Romantic Suspense
Thunder
Rain

Standalone
The Amnesia Project

www.ingramcontent.com/pod-product-compliance
Lightning Source LLC
Chambersburg PA
CBHW020631180626
46816CB00003B/905